ECHOES OF TERROR

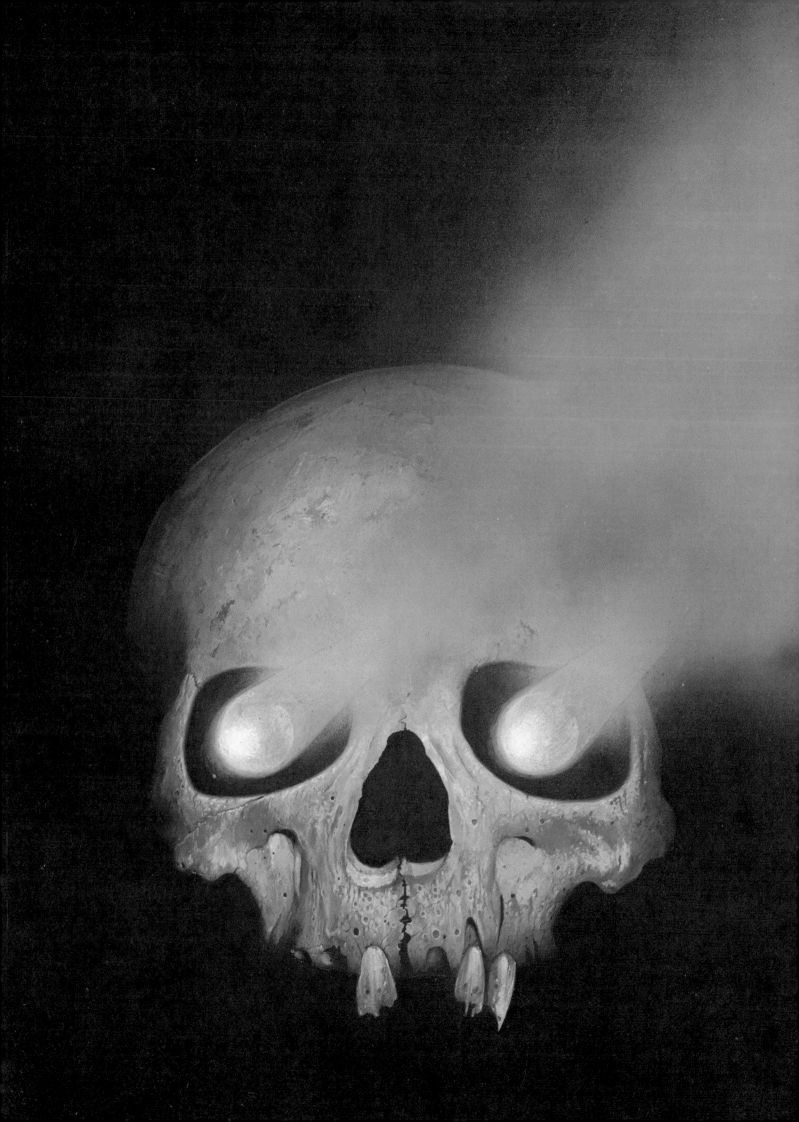

ECHOES OF TERROR

Mike Jarvis & John Spencer
Research by Pete Isaac

Hamlyn
London · New York · Sydney · Toronto

This edition published in 1980 by
The Hamlyn Publishing Group Limited
London · New York · Sydney · Toronto
Astronaut House
Hounslow Road, Feltham, Middlesex

ISBN 0 600 37272 3

Line illustrations by Kathleen McDougall.
Designed by Mike Jarvis
Edited by John Spencer
Typesetting by Bedford Typesetters Limited

Printed in Spain

Contents

Charles Dickens
A Madman's Manuscript   6

Lord Halifax
Three in a Bed   14

Edgar Allan Poe
Masque of the Red Death   16

Bram Stoker
Dracula (an extract)   22

O. Henry
The Furnished Room   32

William Mudford
The Forsaken of God   38

Frederick Marryat
The Werewolf   48

Matthew Lewis
The Midnight Embrace   62

William Makepeace Thackeray
The Devil's Wager   70

W. W. Jacobs
The Monkey's Paw   80

Saki
The Seventh Pullet   90

A Madman's Manuscript
Charles Dickens

Dickens was born in Portsmouth in 1812. After a childhood marred by poverty, a small family inheritance allowed him education sufficient to become a clerk in a lawyer's office. He later distinguished himself as a Parliamentary reporter, and, by the age of thirty, had become phenomenally successful as a writer of fiction. Married since his early twenties, he was, in 1858, separated from his wife, after falling in love with a young actress. He died in 1870, and was buried at Poet's Corner in Westminster Abbey.

'Yes! – a madman's! How that word would have struck to my heart, many years ago! How it would have roused the terror that used to come upon me sometimes, sending the blood hissing and tingling through my veins, till the cold dew of fear stood in large drops upon my skin, and my knees knocked together with fright! I like it now though. It's a fine name. Show me the monarch whose angry frown was ever feared like the glare of a madman's eye – whose cord and axe were ever half so sure as a madman's gripe. Ho! ho! It's a grand thing to be mad! to be peeped at like a wild lion through the iron bars – to gnash one's teeth and howl, through the long still night, to the merry ring of a heavy chain – and to roll and twine among the straw, transported with such brave music. Hurrah for the madhouse! Oh, it's a rare place!

'I remember days when I was *afraid* of being mad; when I used to start from my sleep, and fall upon my knees, and pray to be spared from the curse of my race; when I rushed from the sight of merriment or happiness, to hide myself in some lonely place, and spend the weary hours in watching the progress of the fever that was to consume my brain. I knew that madness was mixed up with my very blood, and the marrow of my bones! that one generation had passed away without the pestilence appearing among them, and that I was the first in whom it would revive. I knew it *must* be so: that so it always had been and so it ever would be: and when I cowered in some obscure corner of a crowded room, and saw men whisper, and point, and turn their eyes towards me, I knew they were telling each other of the doomed madman; and I slunk away again to mope in solitude.

'I did this for years; long, long years they were. The nights here are long sometimes – very long; but they are nothing to the restless nights, and dreadful dreams I had at that time. It makes me cold to remember them. Large dusky forms with sly and jeering faces crouched in the corners of the room, and bent over my bed at night, tempting me to madness. They told me in low whispers, that the floor of the old house in which my father's father died, was stained with his own blood, shed by his own hand in raging madness. I drove my fingers into my ears, but they screamed into my head till the room rang with it, that in one generation before him the madness slumbered, but that his grandfather had lived for years with his hands fettered to the ground, to prevent his tearing himself to pieces. I knew they told the truth – I knew it well. I had found it out years before, though they had tried to keep it from me. Ha! ha! I was too cunning for them, madman as they thought me.

'At last it came upon me, and I wondered how I could ever have feared it. I could go into the world now, and laugh and shout with the best among them. I knew I was mad, but they did not even suspect it. How I used to hug myself with delight, when I thought of the fine trick I was playing them after their old pointing and leering, when I was not mad, but only dreading that I might one day become so! And how I used to laugh for joy, when I was alone, and thought how well I kept my secret, and how quickly my kind friends would have fallen from me, if they had known the truth. I could have screamed with ecstasy when I dined alone with some fine roaring fellow, to think how pale he would have turned, and how fast he would have run, if he had known that the dear friend who sat close to him, sharpening a bright, glittering knife, was a madman with all the power, and half the will, to plunge it in his heart. Oh, it was a merry life!

'Riches became mine, wealth poured in upon me, and I rioted in pleasures enhanced a thousandfold to me by the consciousness of my well-kept secret. I inherited an estate. The law – the eagle-eyed law itself – had been deceived, and had handed over disputed thousands to a madman's hands. Where was the wit of the sharp-sighted men of sound mind? Where the dexterity of the lawyers, eager to discover a flaw? The madman's cunning had overreached them all.

'I had money. How I was courted! I spent it profusely. How I was praised! How those three proud, over-bearing brothers humbled themselves before me! The old, white-headed father, too – such deference – such respect – such devoted friendship – he worshipped me! The old man had a daughter, and the young men a sister; and all the five were poor. I was rich; and when I married the girl, I saw a smile of triumph play upon the faces of her needy relatives, as they thought of their well-planned scheme, and their fine prize. It was for me to smile. To smile! To laugh outright, and tear my hair, and roll upon the ground with shrieks of merriment. They little thought they had married her to a madman.

'Stay. If they had known it, would they have saved her? A sister's happiness against her husband's gold. The lightest feather I blow into the air, against the gay chain that ornaments my body!

'In one thing I was deceived with all my cunning. If I had not been mad – for though we madmen are sharp-witted enough, we get bewildered sometimes – I should have known that the girl would rather have been placed, stiff and cold in a dull leaden coffin, than borne an envied bride to my rich, glittering house, I should have known that her heart was with the dark-eyed boy whose name I once heard her breathe in her troubled sleep; and that she had been sacrificed to me, to relieve the poverty of the old, white-headed man and the haughty brothers.

'I don't remember forms or faces now, but I know the girl was beautiful. I *know* she was; for in the bright moonlight nights, when I start up from my sleep, and all is quiet about me, I see, standing still and motionless in one corner of this cell, a slight and wasted figure with long black hair, which streaming down her back, stirs with no earthly wind, and eyes that fix their gaze on me, and never wink or close. Hush! the blood chills at my heart as I write it down – that form is *hers*; the face is very pale, and the eyes are glassy bright; but I know them well. That figure never moves; it never frowns and mouths as others do, that fill this place sometimes; but it is much more dreadful to me, even than the spirits that tempted me many years ago – it comes fresh from the grave; and is so very death-like.

'For nearly a year I saw that face grow paler; for nearly a year I saw the tears steal down the mournful cheeks, and never knew the cause. I found it out at last though. They could not keep it from me long. She had never liked me; I had never thought she did: she despised my wealth, and hated the splendour in which she lived; but I had not expected that. She loved another. This I had never thought of. Strange feelings came over me, and thought, forced upon me by some secret power, whirled round and round my brain. I did not hate her, though I hated the boy she still wept for. I pitied – yes, I pitied – the wretched life to which her cold and selfish relations had doomed her. I knew that she could not live long; but the thought that before her death she might give birth to some ill-fated being, destined to hand down madness to its offspring, determined me. I resolved to kill her.

'For many weeks I thought of poison, and then of drowning, and then of fire. A fine sight, the grand house in flames, and the madman's wife smouldering away to cinders. Think of the jest of a large reward, too, and of some sane man swinging in the wind for a deed he never did, and all through a madman's cunning! I thought often of this, but I gave it up at last. Oh! the pleasure of stropping the razor day after day, feeling the sharp edge, and thinking of the gash one stroke of its thin, bright edge would make!

'At last the old spirits who had been with me so often before whispered in my ear that the time was come,

and thrust the open razor into my hand. I grasped it firmly, rose softly from the bed, and leaned over my sleeping wife. Her face was buried in her hands. I withdrew them softly, and they fell listlessly on her bosom. She had been weeping; for the traces of the tears were still wet upon her cheek. Her face was calm and placid; and even as I looked upon it, a tranquil smile lighted up her pale features. I laid my hand softly on her shoulder. She started – it was only a passing dream. I leaned forward again. She screamed, and woke.

'One motion of my hand, and she would never again have uttered cry or sound. But I was startled, and drew back. Her eyes were fixed on mine. I knew not how it was, but they cowed and frightened me; and I quailed beneath them. She rose from the bed, still gazing fixedly and steadily on me. I trembled; the razor was in my hand, but I could not move. She made towards the door. As she neared it, she turned, and withdrew her eyes from my face. The spell was broken. I bounded forward, and clutched her by the arm. Uttering shriek upon shriek, she sank upon the ground.

'Now I could have killed her without a struggle; but the house was alarmed. I heard the tread of footsteps on the stairs. I replaced the razor in its usual drawer, unfastened the door, and called loudly for assistance.

'They came, and raised her, and placed her on the bed. She lay bereft of animation for hours; and when life, look, and speech returned, her senses had deserted her, and she raved wildly and furiously.

'Doctors were called in – great men who rolled up to my door in easy carriages, with fine horses and gaudy servants. They were at her bedside for weeks. They had a great meeting, and consulted together in low and solemn voices in another room. One, the cleverest and most celebrated among them, took me aside, and bidding me prepare for the worst, told me – me, the madman! – that my wife was mad. He stood close beside me at an open window, his eyes looking in my face, and his hand laid upon my arm. With one effort, I could have hurled him into the street beneath. It would have been rare sport to have done it; but my secret was at stake, and I let him go. A few days after, they told me I must place her under some restraint: I must provide a keeper for her. *I*! I went into the open fields where none could hear me, and laughed till the air resounded with my shouts!

'She died next day. The white-headed old man followed her to the grave, and the proud brothers dropped a tear over the insensible corpse of her whose sufferings they had regarded in her lifetime with muscles of iron. All this was food for my secret mirth, and I laughed behind the white handkerchief which I held up to my face, as we rode home, till the tears came into my eyes.

'But though I had carried my object and killed her, I was restless and disturbed, and I felt that before long my secret must be known. I could not hide the wild mirth and joy which boiled within me, and made me when I was alone, at home, jump up and beat my hands together, and dance round and round, and roar aloud. When I went out, and saw the busy crowds hurrying about the street; or, to the theatre, and heard the sound of music, and beheld the people dancing, I felt such glee, that I could have rushed among them, and torn them to pieces limb from limb, and howled in transport. But I ground my teeth, and struck my feet upon the floor, and drove my sharp nails into my hands. I kept it down; and no one knew I was a madman yet.

'I remember – though it's one of the last things I *can* remember: for now I mix up realities with my dreams, and having so much to do, and being always hurried here, have no time to separate the two, from some strange confusion in which they get involved – I remember how I let it out at last. Ha! ha! I think I see their frightened looks now, and feel the ease with which I flung them from me, and dashed my clenched fist into their white faces, and then flew like the wind, and left them screaming and shouting far behind. The strength of a giant comes upon me when I think of it. There – see how this iron bar bends beneath my furious wrench. I could snap it like a twig, only there are long galleries here with many doors – I don't think I could find my way along them; and even if I could, I know there are iron gates below which they keep locked and barred. They know what a clever madman I have been, and they are proud to have me here, to show.

'Let me see: yes, I had been out. It was late at night when I reached home, and found the proudest of the three proud brothers waiting to see me – urgent business he said: I recollect it well. I hated that man with all a madman's hate. Many and many a time had my fingers longed to tear him. They told me he was there. I ran swiftly upstairs. He had a word to say to me. I dismissed the servants. It was late, and we were alone together – *for the first time.*

'I kept my eyes carefully from him at first, for I knew what he little thought – and I gloried in the knowledge – that the light of madness gleamed from them like fire. We sat in silence for a few minutes. He spoke at last. My recent dissipation, and strange remarks, made so soon after his sister's death, were an insult to her memory. Coupling together many circumstances which had at first escaped his observation, he thought I had not treated

her well. He wished to know whether he was right in inferring that I meant to cast a reproach upon her memory, and a disrespect upon her family. It was due to the uniform he wore to demand this explanation.

'This man had a commission in the army – a commission, purchased with my money, and his sister's misery! This was the man who had been foremost in the plot to ensnare me, and grasp my wealth. This was the man who had been the main instrument in forcing his sister to wed me; well knowing that her heart was given to that puling boy. Due to *his* uniform! The livery of his degradation! I turned my eyes upon him – I could not help it – but I spoke not a word.

'I saw the sudden change that came upon him beneath my gaze. He was a bold man, but the colour faded from his face, and he drew back in his chair. I dragged mine nearer to him; and as I laughed – I was very merry then – I saw him shudder. I felt the madness rising within me. He was afraid of me.

' "You were very fond of your sister when she was alive," I said. – "Very."

'He looked uneasily round him, and I saw his hand grasp the back of his chair; but he said nothing.

' "You villain," said I, "I found you out; I discovered your hellish plots against me; I know her heart was fixed on some one else before you compelled her to marry me. I know it – I know it."

'He jumped suddenly from his chair, brandishing it aloft, and bid me stand back – for I took care to be getting closer to him all the time I spoke.

'I screamed rather than talked, for I felt tumultuous passions eddying through my veins, and the old spirits whispering and taunting me to tear his heart out.

' "Damn you," said I, starting up, and rushing upon him; "I killed her. I am a madman. Down with you. Blood, blood! I will have it!"

'I turned aside with one blow the chair he hurled at me in his terror, and closed with him; and with a heavy crash we rolled upon the floor together.

'It was a fine struggle that; for he was a tall, strong man, fighting for his life; and I, a powerful madman, thirsting to destroy him. I knew no strength could equal mine, and I was right. Right again, though a madman! His struggles grew fainter. I knelt upon his chest, and clasped his brawny throat firmly with both hands. His face grew purple; his eyes were starting from his head, and with protruded tongue, he seemed to mock me. I squeezed the tighter.

'The door was suddenly burst open with a loud noise, and a crowd of people rushed forward, crying aloud to each other to secure the madman.

'My secret was out; and my only struggle now was for liberty and freedom. I gained my feet before a hand was on me, threw myself among my assailants, and cleared my way with my strong arm, as if I bore a hatchet in my hand, and hewed them down before me. I gained the door, dropped over the banisters, and in an instant was in the street.

'Straight and swift I ran, and no one dared to stop me, I heard the noise of feet behind, and redoubled my speed. It grew fainter and fainter in the distance, and at length died away altogether; but on I bounded, through marsh and rivulet, over fence and wall, with a wild shout which was taken up by the strange beings that flocked around me on every side, and swelled the sound, till it pierced the air. I was borne upon the arms of demons who swept along upon the wind, and bore down bank and hedge before them, and spun me round and round with a rustle and a speed that made my head swim, until at last they threw me from them with a violent shock, and I fell heavily upon the earth. When I woke I found myself here – here in this gay cell, where the sunlight seldom comes, and the moon steals in, in rays which only serve to show the dark shadows about me, and that silent figure in its old corner. When I lie awake, I can sometimes hear strange shrieks and cries from distant parts of this large place. What they are, I know not; but they neither come from that pale form, nor does it regard them. For from the first shades of dusk till the earliest light of morning, it still stands motionless in the same place, listening to the music of my iron chain, and watching my gambols on my straw bed.'

Three in a Bed
Lord Halifax

Sir Charles Lindley Wood, fourth baronet and Second Viscount Halifax

Lord Halifax was born in London in 1839. Educated at Eton and Oxford, he subsequently served in the Royal Household, and was active in the Red Cross during the Crimean War. His main interest was in the controversial Oxford movement of the Church of England, and he was at the centre of many legal storms. Although not active in politics, as President of the Church Union, he wielded great influence in England. He died in 1934.

A certain minister and his wife took a large house near a town in one of the Eastern counties. After they had been there a little while, they were disquieted to observe that, although they were not using the upper floor of the house, often when they came home at night after evening service, they used to see lights in the upper windows.

One day, an old friend came to stay with them, and since there was no other accommodation, they put him to sleep in one of the rooms on the top floor. After his first night, the visitor came down to breakfast looking pale and harassed. He found that he had to leave at once, and although they pressed him to remain, nothing would shake his determination, nor, although they questioned him, would he give any explanation of his sudden change of plan.

A little later on, a young couple arrived as guests. They were given the same room as the previous visitor. When they retired to bed there was a bright fire burning and there was nothing to disquiet them. They settled themselves for the night and soon fell asleep. Presently the man awoke with a start and a strong feeling that he was lying between two people. So certain was he of this that he dared not put out his hand on the side opposite to that on which his wife was lying. Instead, very cautiously, he roused his wife, and persuaded her to get out of the bed on the far side. He followed her, and then, looking back, they both distinctly saw, by the light of the fire, the bedclothes heaped up round a human form which lay in the bed.

As they stared, they heard footsteps coming slowly and softly down the passage outside. After a moment's pause, the brass handle turned and the door, which had been locked, swung open. The unfortunate couple hid their eyes in terror, so they saw nothing of what immediately followed. But they heard the footsteps pad softly across the room. There was silence, and then a dreadful gurgle; and looking at the bed once more, they saw the clothes twitched suddenly right off it on to the floor. The footsteps retreated to the door then died away down the passage.

The rest of the night was spent in fear and watchfulness; and when, next morning, the maid arrived with their hot water, the door was still locked. Coming down to breakfast in great agitation, they told their experience to their host, who wrote off at once to his previous visitor. The latter replied that he had had a precisely similar experience. No explanation of any kind was forthcoming, and the house was given up.

Masque of the Red Death
Edgar Allan Poe

Poe was born in Boston in 1809. When his mother died in 1811, he was adopted into the family of John Allan, from whom he took his middle name. He was expelled from university because of gambling debts, and dismissed from West Point Academy for excessive drinking. In 1836 he married a girl of thirteen. When she died, in 1847, the shock of her death combined with his excessive drinking led directly to his own premature death two years later.

The 'Red Death' had long devastated the country. No pestilence had ever been so fatal, or so hideous. Blood was its Avatar and its seal – the redness and horror of blood. There were sharp pains, and sudden dizziness, and then profuse bleeding at the pores, with dissolution. The scarlet stains upon the body and especially upon the face of the victim, were the pest ban which shut him out from the aid and from the sympathy of his fellow-men. And the whole seizure, progress, and termination of the disease, were the incidents of half an hour.

But the Prince Prospero was happy and dauntless and sagacious. When his dominions were half-depopulated, he summoned to his presence a thousand hale and light-hearted friends from among the knights and dames of his court, and with these retired to the deep seclusion of one of his castellated abbeys. This was an extensive and magnificent structure, the creation of the prince's own eccentric yet august taste. A strong and lofty wall girdled it in. This wall had gates of iron. The courtiers, having entered, brought furnaces and massy hammers and welded the bolts. They resolved to leave means neither of ingress nor egress to the sudden impulses of despair or of frenzy from within. The abbey was amply provisioned. With such precautions the courtiers might bid defiance to contagion. The external world could take care of itself. In the meantime it was folly to grieve, or to think. The prince had provided all the appliances of pleasure. There were buffoons, there were improvisatori, there were ballet-dancers, there were musicians, there was Beauty, there was wine. All these and security were within. Without was the 'Red Death.'

It was toward the close of the fifth or sixth month of his seclusion, and while the pestilence raged most furiously abroad, that the Prince Prospero entertained his thousand friends at a masked ball of the most unusual magnificence.

It was a voluptuous scene, that masquerade. But first let me tell of the rooms in which it was held. These were seven – an imperial suite. In many palaces, however, such suites form a long and straight vista, while the folding doors slide back nearly to the walls on either hand, so that the view of the whole extent is scarcely impeded. Here the case was very different, as might have been expected from the duke's love of the *bizarre*. The apartments were so irregularly disposed that the vision embraced but little more than one at a time. There was a sharp turn at every twenty or thirty yards, and at each turn a novel effect. To the right and left, in the middle of each wall, a tall and narrow Gothic window looked out upon a closed corridor which pursued the windings of the suite. These windows were of stained glass whose colour varied in accordance with the pre-

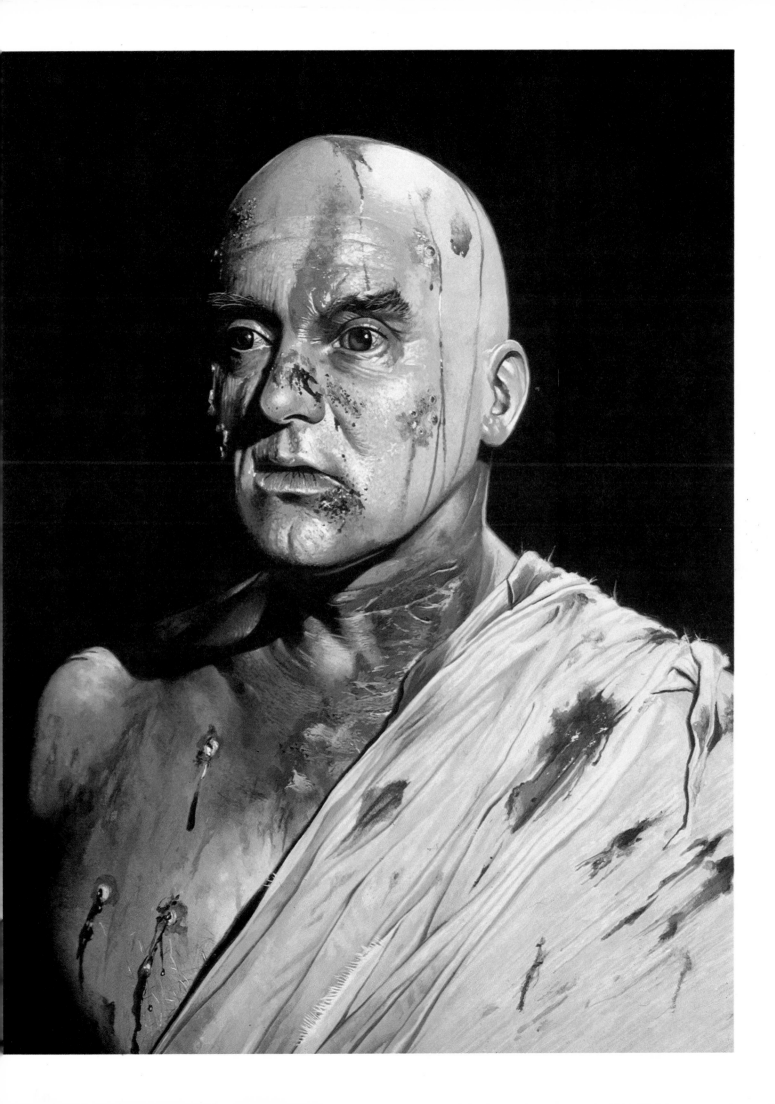

vailing hue of the decorations of the chamber into which it opened. That at the eastern extremity was hung, for example, in blue – and vividly blue were its windows. The second chamber was purple in its ornaments and tapestries, and here the panes were purple. The third was green throughout, and so were the casements. The fourth was furnished and lighted with orange – the fifth with white – the sixth with violet. The seventh apartment was closely shrouded in black velvet tapestries that hung all over the ceiling and down the walls, falling in heavy folds upon a carpet of the same material and hue. But in this chamber only, the colour of the windows failed to correspond with the decorations. The panes here were scarlet – a deep blood colour. Now in no one of the seven apartments was there any lamp or candelabrum, amid the profusion of golden ornaments that lay scattered to and fro or depended from the roof. There was no light of any kind emanating from lamp or candle within the suite of chambers. But in the corridors that followed the suite there stood, opposite to each window, a heavy tripod, bearing a brazier of fire, that projected its rays through the tinted glass and so glaringly illumined the room. And thus were produced a multitude of gaudy and fantastic appearances. But in the western or black chamber the effect of the fire-light that streamed upon the dark hangings through the blood-tinted panes was ghastly in the extreme, and produced so wild a look upon the countenances of those who entered, that there were few of the company bold enough to set foot within its precincts at all.

It was in this apartment, also, that there stood against the western wall, a gigantic clock of ebony. Its pendulum swung to and fro with a dull, heavy, monotonous clang; and when the minute-hand made the circuit of the face, and the hour was to be stricken, there came from the brazen lungs of the clock a sound which was clear and loud and deep and exceedingly musical, but of so peculiar a note and emphasis that, at each lapse of an hour, the musicians of the orchestra were constrained to pause, momentarily, in their performance, to harken to the sound; and thus the waltzers perforce ceased their evolutions; and there was a brief disconcert of the whole gay company; and, while the chimes of the clock yet rang, it was observed that the giddiest grew pale, and the more aged and sedate passed their hands over their brows as if in confused reverie or meditation. But when the echoes had fully ceased, a light laughter at once pervaded the assembly; the musicians looked at each other and smiled as if at their own nervousness and folly, and made whispering vows, each to the other, that the next chiming of the clock should produce in them no similar emotion; and then, after the lapse of sixty minutes (which embrace three thousand and six hundred seconds of the Time that flies), there came yet another chiming of the clock, and then were the same disconcert and tremulousness and meditation as before.

But, in spite of these things, it was a gay and magnificent revel. The tastes of the duke were peculiar. He had a fine eye for colours and effects. He disregarded the *decora* of mere fashion. His plans were bold and fiery, and his conceptions glowed with barbaric lustre. There are some who would have thought him mad. His followers felt that he was not. It was necessary to hear and see and touch him to be *sure* that he was not.

He had directed, in great part, the movable embellishments of the seven chambers, upon occasion of this great *fête*; and it was his own guiding taste which had given character to the masqueraders. Be sure they were grotesque. There were much glare and glitter and piquancy and phantasm – much of what has been since seen in *Hernani*. There were arabesque figures with unsuited limbs and appointments. There were delirious fancies such as the madman fashions. There were much of the beautiful, much of the wanton, much of the *bizarre*, something of the terrible, and not a little of that which might have excited disgust. To and fro in the seven chambers there stalked, in fact, a multitude of dreams. And these – the dreams – writhed in and about, taking hue from the rooms, and causing the wild music of the orchestra to seem as the echo of their steps. And, anon, there strikes the ebony clock which stands in the hall of the velvet. And then, for a moment, all is still, and all is silent save the voice of the clock. The dreams are stiff-frozen as they stand. But the echoes of the chime die away – they have endured but an instant – and a light, half-subdued laughter floats after them as they depart. And now again the music swells, and the dreams live, and writhe to and fro more merrily than ever, taking hue from the many-tinted windows through which stream the rays from the tripods. But to the chamber which lies most westwardly of the seven there are now none of the maskers who venture; for the night is waning away; and there flows a ruddier light through the blood-coloured panes; and the blackness of the sable drapery appals; and to him whose foot falls upon the sable carpet, there comes from the near clock of ebony a muffled peal more solemnly emphatic than any which reaches *their* ears who indulged in the more remote gaieties of the other apartments.

But these other apartments were densely crowded, and in them beat feverishly the heart of life. And the revel went whirlingly on, until at length there commenced the sounding of midnight upon the clock. And then

the music ceased, as I have told; and the evolutions of the waltzers were quieted; and there was an uneasy cessation of all things as before. But now there were twelve strokes to be sounded by the bell of the clock; and thus it happened, perhaps, that more of thought crept, with more of time, into the meditations of the thoughtful among those who revelled. And thus too, it happened, perhaps, that before the last echoes of the last chime had utterly sunk into silence, there were many individuals in the crowd who had found leisure to become aware of the presence of a masked figure which had arrested the attention of no single individual before. And the rumour of this new presence having spread itself whisperingly around, there arose at length from the whole company a buzz, or murmur, expressive of disapprobation and surprise – then, finally, of terror, of horror, and of disgust.

In an assembly of phantasms such as I have painted, it may well be supposed that no ordinary appearance could have excited such sensation. In truth the masquerade licence of the night was nearly unlimited; but the figure in question had out-Heroded Herod, and gone beyond the bounds of even the prince's indefinite decorum. There are chords in the hearts of the most reckless which cannot be touched without emotion. Even with the utterly lost, to whom life and death are equally jests, there are matters of which no jest can be made. The whole company, indeed, seemed now deeply to feel that in the costume and bearing of the stranger neither wit nor propriety existed. The figure was tall and gaunt, and shrouded from head to foot in the habiliments of the grave. The mask which concealed the visage was made so nearly to resemble the countenance of a stiffened corpse that the closest scrutiny must have had difficulty in detecting the cheat. And yet all this might have been endured, if not approved, by the mad revellers around. But the mummer had gone so far as to assume the type of the Red Death. His vesture was dabbled in *blood* – and his broad brow, with all the features of the face, was sprinkled with the scarlet horror.

When the eyes of Prince Prospero fell upon this spectral image (which, with a slow and solemn movement, as if more fully to sustain its *rôle*, stalked to and fro among the waltzers) he was seen to be convulsed in the first moment with a strong shudder either of terror or distaste; but, in the next, his brow reddened with rage.

'Who dares,' – he demanded hoarsely of the courtiers who stood near him – 'who dares insult us with this blasphemous mockery? Seize him and unmask him – that we may know whom we have to hang, at sunrise, from the battlements!'

It was in the eastern or blue chamber in which stood the Prince Prospero as he uttered these words. They rang throughout the seven rooms loudly and clearly, for the prince was a bold and robust man, and the music had become hushed at the waving of his hand.

It was in the blue room where stood the prince, with a group of pale courtiers by his side. At first, as he spoke, there was a slight rushing movement of this group in the direction of the intruder, who at the moment was also near at hand, and now, with deliberate and stately step, made closer approach to the speaker. But from a certain nameless awe with which the mad assumptions of the mummer had inspired the whole party, there were found none who put forth hand to seize him; so that, unimpeded, he passed within a yard of the prince's person; and, while the vast assembly, as if with one impulse, shrank from the centres of the rooms to the walls, he made his way uninterruptedly, but with the same solemn and measured step which had distinguished him from the first, through the blue chamber to the purple – through the purple to the green – through the green to the orange – through this again to the white – and even thence to the violet, ere a decided movement had been made to arrest him. It was then, however, that the Prince Prospero, maddening with rage and the shame of his own momentary cowardice, rushed hurriedly through the six chambers, while none followed him on account of a deadly terror that had seized upon all. He bore aloft a drawn dagger, and had approached, in rapid impetuosity, to within three or four feet of the retreating figure, when the latter, having attained the extremity of the velvet apartment, turned suddenly and confronted his pursuer. There was a sharp cry – and the dagger dropped gleaming upon the sable carpet, upon which, instantly afterward, fell prostrate in death the Prince Prospero. Then, summoning the wild courage of despair, a throng of the revellers at once threw themselves into the black apartment, and, seizing the mummer, whose tall figure stood erect and motionless within the shadow of the ebony clock, gasped in unutterable horror at finding the grave cerements and corpse-like mask, which they handled with so violent a rudeness, untenanted by any tangible form.

And now was acknowledged the presence of the Red Death. He had come like a thief in the night. And one by one dropped the revellers in the blood-bedewed halls of their revel, and died each in the despairing posture of his fall. And the life of the ebony clock went out with that of the last of the gay. And the flames of the tripods expired. And Darkness and Decay and the Red Death held illimitable dominion over all.

Dracula
(An extract)
Bram Stoker

Bram Stoker was born in Dublin in 1847, and was educated at Trinity College where he was successful both academically, and as an athlete, despite having been an invalid as a child. An Irish Civil servant for ten years, his first publication was 'The Duties of Clerks of Petty Sessions in Ireland.' From 1847 he became manager of Henry Irving's Theatre, The Lyceum. Stoker wrote many novels but his only major success was Dracula, which was published in 1897. He died in 1912.

When I found that I was a prisoner a sort of wild feeling came over me. I rushed up and down the stairs, trying every door and peering out of every window I could find; but after a little the conviction of my helplessness overpowered all other things. When I look back after a few hours I think I must have been mad for the time, for I behaved much as a rat does in a trap. When, however, the conviction had come to me that I was helpless I sat down quietly – as quietly as I have ever done anything in my life – and began to think over what was best to be done. I am thinking still, and as yet have come to no definite conclusion. Of one thing only am I certain: that it is no use making my ideas known to the Count. He knows well that I am imprisoned; and as he has done it himself, and has doubtless his own motives for it, he would only deceive me if I trusted him fully with the facts. So far as I can see, my only plan will be to keep my knowledge and my fears to myself, and my eyes open. I am, I know, either being deceived, like a baby, by my own fears, or else I am in desperate straits; and if the latter be so, I need, and shall need, all my brains to get through. I had hardly come to this conclusion when I heard the great door below shut, and knew that the Count had returned. He did not come at once into the library, so I went cautiously to my own room and found him making the bed. This was odd, but only confirmed what I had all along thought – that there were no servants in the house. When later I saw him through the chink of the hinges of the door laying the table in the dining-room, I was assured of it; for if he does himself all these menial offices, surely it is proof that there is no one else to do them. This gave me a fright, for if there is no one else in the castle, it must have been the Count himself who was the driver of the coach that brought me here. This is a terrible thought; for if so, what does it mean that he could control the wolves, as he did, by only holding up his hand in silence? How was it that all the people at Bistritz and on the coach had some terrible fear for me? What meant the giving of the crucifix, of the garlic, of the wild rose, of the mountain ash? Bless that good, good woman who hung the crucifix round my neck! for it is a comfort and a strength to me whenever I touch it. It is odd that a thing which I have been taught to regard with disfavour and as idolatrous should in a time of loneliness and trouble be of help. Is it that there is something in the essence of the thing itself, or that it is a medium, a tangible help, in conveying memories of sympathy and comfort? Some time, if it may be, I must examine this matter and try to make up my mind about it. In the meantime I must find out all I can about Count Dracula, as it may help me to understand. To-night he may talk of himself, if I turn the conversation that way. I must be very careful, however, not to awake his suspicion.

Midnight. – I have had a long talk with the Count. I asked him a few questions on Transylvanian history,· and he warmed up to the subject wonderfully. In his speaking of things and people, and especially of battles, he spoke as if he had been present at them all. This he afterwards explained by saying that to a *boyar* the pride of his house and name is his own pride, that their glory is his glory, that their fate is his fate. Whenever he spoke of his house he always said 'we,' and spoke almost in the plural, like a king speaking. I wish I could put down all he said exactly as he said it, for to me it was most fascinating. It seemed to have in it a whole history of the country. He grew excited as he spoke, and walked about the room pulling his great white moustache and grasping anything on which he laid his hands as though he would crush it by main strength. One thing he said which I shall put down as nearly as I can; for it tells in its way the story of his race: –

'We Szekelys have a right to be proud, for in our veins flows the blood of many brave races who fought as the lion fights, for lordship. Here, in the whirlpool of European races, the Ugric tribe bore down from Iceland the fighting spirit which Thor and Wodin gave them, which their Berserkers displayed to such fell intent on the seaboards of Europe, aye, and of Asia and Africa, too, till the peoples thought that the were-wolves themselves had come. Here, too, when they came, they found the Huns, whose warlike fury had swept the earth like a living flame, till the dying peoples held that in their veins ran the blood of those old witches, who, expelled from Scythia, had mated with the devils in the desert. Fools, fools! What devil or what witch was ever so great as Attila, whose blood is in these veins?' He held up his arms. 'Is it a wonder that we were a conquering race; that we were proud; that when the Magyar, the Lombard, the Avar, the Bulgar, or the Turk poured his thousands on our frontiers, we drove them back? Is it strange that when Arpad and his legions swept through the Hungarian fatherland he found us here when he reached the frontier; that the Honfoglalas was completed there? And when the Hungarian flood swept eastward, the Szekelys were claimed as kindred by the victorious Magyars, and to us for centuries was trusted the guarding of the frontier of Turkey-land; aye, and more than that, endless duty of the frontier guard, for, as the Turks say, 'water sleeps, and enemy is sleepless.' Who more gladly than we throughout the Four Nations received the 'bloody sword,' or at its warlike call flocked quicker to the standard of the King? When was redeemed that great shame of my nation, the shame of Cassova, when the flags of the Wallach and the Magyar went down beneath the Crescent; who was it but one of my own race who as Voivode crossed the Danube and beat the Turk on his own ground! This was a Dracula indeed. Who was it that his own unworthy brother, when he had fallen, sold his people to the Turk and brought the shame of slavery on them! Was it not this Dracula, indeed, who inspired that other of his race who in a later age again and again brought his forces over the great river into Turkey-land; who, when he was beaten back, came again, and again, and again, though he had to come alone from the bloody field where his troops were being slaughtered, since he knew that he alone could ultimately triumph? They said that he thought only of himself. Bah! what good are peasants without a leader? Where ends the war without a brain and heart to conduct it? Again, when, after the battle of Mohacs, we threw off the Hungarian yoke, we of the Dracula blood were amongst their leaders, for our spirit would not brook that we were not free. Ah, young sir, the Szekelys – and the Dracula as their heart's blood, their brains, and their swords – can boast a record that mushroom growths like the Hapsburgs and the Romanoffs can never reach. The warlike days are over. Blood is too precious a thing in these days of dishonourable peace; and the glories of the great races are as a tale that is told.'

It was by this time close on morning, and we went to bed. (*Mem.*, this diary seems horribly like the beginning of the 'Arabian Nights,' for everything has to break off at cockcrow – or like the ghost of Hamlet's father.)

12 May. – Let me begin with facts – bare, meagre facts, verified by books and figures, and of which there can be no doubt. I must not confuse them with experiences which will have to rest on my own observation or my memory of them. Last evening when the Count came from his room he began by asking me questions on legal matters and on the doing of certain kinds of business. I had spent the day wearily over books, and, simply to keep my mind occupied, went over some of the matters I had been examined in at Lincoln's Inn. There was a certain method in the Count's inquiries, so I shall try to put them down in sequence; the knowledge may somehow or some time be useful to me.

First, he asked if a man in England might have two solicitors, or more. I told him he might have a dozen if he wished, but that it would not be wise to have more than one solicitor engaged in one transaction, as only one could act at a time, and that to change would be certain to militate against his interest. He seemed thoroughly to understand, and went on to ask if there would be any practical difficulty in having one man to attend, say, to banking, and another to look after shipping, in case local help were needed in a place far from the home of the banking solicitor. I asked him to explain more fully, so that I might not by any chance mislead him, so he said: –

'I shall illustrate. Your friend and mine, Mr. Peter Hawkins, from under the shadow of your beautiful cathedral at Exeter, which is far from London, buys for me through your good self my place at London. Good! Now here let me say frankly, lest you should think it strange that I have sought the services of one so far off from London instead of someone resident there, that my motive was that no local interest might be served save my wish only; and as one of London resident might, perhaps, have some purpose of himself or friend to serve I went thus afield to seek my agent, whose labours should be only to my interest. Now, suppose I, who have much of affairs, wish to ship goods, say, to Newcastle, or Durham, or Harwich, or Dover, might it not be that it could with more ease be done by consigning to one in these ports?' I answered that certainly it would be most easy, but that we solicitors had a system of agency one for the other, so that local work could be done locally on instruction from any solicitor, so that the client, simply placing himself in the hands of one man, could have his wishes carried out by him without further trouble.

'But,' said he, 'I could be at liberty to direct myself. Is it not so?'

'Of course,' I replied; 'and such is often done by men of business, who do not like the whole of their affairs to be known by any one person.'

'Good!' he said, and then went on to ask about the means of making consignments and the forms to be gone through, and of all sorts of difficulties which might arise, but by forethought could be guarded against. I explained all these things to him to the best of my ability, and he certainly left me under the impression that he would have made a wonderful solicitor, for there was nothing that he did not think of or foresee. For a man who was never in the country, and who did not evidently do much in the way of business, his knowledge and acumen were wonderful. When he had satisfied himself on these points of which he had spoken, and I had verified all as well as I could by the books available, he suddenly stood up and said: –

'Have you written since your first letter to our friend Mr. Peter Hawkins, or to any other?' It was with some bitterness in my heart that I answered that I had not, that as yet I had not seen any opportunity of sending letters to anybody.

'Then write now, my young friend,' he said, laying a heavy hand on my shoulder; 'write to our friend and to any other; and say, if it will please you, that you shall stay with me until a month from now.'

'Do you wish me to stay so long?' I asked, for my heart grew cold at the thought.

'I desire it much; nay, I will take no refusal. When your master, employer, what you will, engaged that some-one should come on his behalf, it was understood that my needs only were to be consulted. I have not stinted. Is it not so?'

What could I do but bow acceptance? It was Mr. Hawkins's interest, not mine, and I had to think of him, not myself; and besides, while Count Dracula was speaking, there was that in his eyes and in his bearing which made me remember that I was a prisoner, and that if I wished it I could have no choice. The Count saw his victory in my bow, and his mastery in the trouble of my face, for he began at once to use them, but in his own smooth, resistless way: –

'I pray you, my good young friend, that you will not discourse of things other than business in your letters. It will doubtless please your friends to know that you are well, and that you look forward to getting home to them. Is it not so?' As he spoke he handed me three sheets of notepaper and three envelopes. They were all of the thinnest foreign post, and looking at them, then at him, and noticing his quiet smile, with the sharp, canine teeth lying over the red under-lip, I understood as well as if he had spoken that I should be careful what I wrote, for he would be able to read it. So I determined to write only formal notes now, but to write fully to Mr. Hawkins in secret, and also to Mina, for to her I could write in shorthand, which would puzzle the Count, if he did see it. When I had written my two letters I sat quiet, reading a book whilst the Count wrote several notes, referring as he wrote them to some books on his table. Then he took up my two and placed them with his own, and put by his writing materials, after which, the instant the door had closed behind him, I leaned over and looked at the letters, which were face down on the table. I felt no compunction in doing so, for under the circumstances I felt that I should protect myself in every way I could.

One of the letters was directed to Samuel F. Billington, No. 7, The Crescent, Whitby; another to Herr Leutner, Varna; the third was to Coutts & Co., London, and the fourth to Herren Klopstock & Billreuth, bankers, Buda-Pesth. The second and fourth were unsealed. I was just about to look at them when I saw the doorhandle move. I sank back in my seat, having just had time to replace the letters as they had been and to resume my book before the Count, holding still another letter in his hand, entered the room. He took up the letters on the table and stamped them carefully, and then, turning to me, said: –

'I trust you will forgive me, but I have much work to do in private this evening. You will, I hope, find all things as you wish.' At the door he turned, and after a moment's pause said:

'Let me advise you, my dear young friend – nay, let me warn you with all seriousness, that should you leave these rooms you will not by any chance go to sleep in any other part of the castle. It is old, and has many memories, and there are bad dreams for those who sleep unwisely. Be warned! Should sleep now or ever overcome you, or be like to do, then haste to your own chamber or to these rooms, for your rest will then be safe. But if you be not careful in this respect, then –' He finished his speech in a gruesome way, for he motioned with his hands as if he were washing them. I quite understood; my only doubt was as to whether any dream could be more terrible than the unnatural, horrible net of gloom and mystery which seemed closing round me.

Later. – I endorse the last words written, but this time there is no doubt in question. I shall not fear to sleep in any place where he is not. I have placed the crucifix over the head of my bed – I imagine that my rest is thus freer from dreams; and there it shall remain.

When he left me I went to my room. After a little while, not hearing any sound, I came out and went up the stone stair to where I could look out towards the south. There was some sense of freedom in the vast expanse, inaccessible though it was to me, as compared with the narrow darkness of the courtyard. Looking out on this, I felt that I was indeed in prison, and I seemed to want a breath of fresh air, though it were of the night. I am beginning to feel this nocturnal existence tell on me. It is destroying my nerve. I start at my own shadow, and am full of all sorts of horrible imaginings. God knows that there is ground for any terrible fear in this accursed place! I looked out over the beautiful expanse, bathed in soft yellow moonlight till it was almost as light as day. In the soft light the distant hills became melted, and the shadows in the valleys and gorges of velvety blackness. The mere beauty seemed to cheer me; there was peace and comfort in every breath I drew. As I leaned from the window my eye was caught by something moving a story below me, and somewhat to my left, where I imagined, from the lie of the rooms, that the windows of the Count's own room would look out. The window at which I stood was tall and deep, stone-mullioned, and though weather-worn, was still complete; but it was evidently many a day since the case had been there. I drew back behind the stonework, and looked carefully out.

What I saw was the Count's head coming out from the window. I did not see the face, but I knew the man by the neck and the movement of his back and arms. In any case, I could not mistake the hands which I had had so many opportunities of studying. I was at first interested and somewhat amused, for it is wonderful how small a matter will interest and amuse a man when he is a prisoner. But my very feelings changed to repulsion and terror when I saw the whole man slowly emerge from the window and begin to crawl down the castle wall over that dreadful abyss, *face down*, with his cloak spreading out around him like great wings. At first I could not believe my eyes. I thought it was some trick of the moonlight, some weird effect of shadow; but I kept looking, and it could be no delusion. I saw the fingers and toes grasp the corners of the stones, worn clear of the mortar by the stress of years, and by thus using every projection and inequality move downwards with considerable speed, just as a lizard moves along a wall.

What manner of man is this, or what manner of creature is it in the semblance of man? I feel the dread of this horrible place overpowering me; I am in fear – in awful fear – and there is no escape for me; I am encompassed about with terrors that I dare not think of. . . .

15 May. – Once more have I seen the Count go out in his lizard fashion. He moved downwards in a sidelong way, some hundred feet down, and a good deal to the left. He vanished into some hole or window. When his head had disappeared I leaned out to try and see more, but without avail – the distance was too great to allow a proper angle of sight. I knew he had left the castle now, and thought to use the opportunity to explore more than I had dared to do as yet. I went back to the room, and taking a lamp, tried all the doors. They were all locked as I had expected, and the locks were comparatively new; but I went down the stone stairs to the hall where I had entered originally. I found I could pull back the bolts easily enough and unhook the great chains; but the door was locked, and the key was gone! That key must be in the Count's room; I must watch should his door be unlocked, so that I may get it and escape. I went on to make a thorough examination of the

various stairs and passages, and to try the doors that opened from them. One or two small rooms near the hall were open, but there was nothing to see in them except old furniture, dusty with age and moth-eaten. At last, however, I found one door at the top of a stairway which, though it seemed to be locked, gave a little under pressure. I tried it harder, and found that it was not really locked, but that the resistance came from the fact that the hinges had fallen somewhat, and the heavy door rested on the floor. Here was an opportunity which I might not have again, so I exerted myself, and with many efforts forced it back so that I could enter. I was now in a wing of the castle further to the right than the rooms I knew and a story lower down. From the windows I could see that the suite of rooms lay along to the south of the castle, the windows of the end room looking out both west and south. On the latter side, as well as to the former, there was a great precipice. The castle was built on the corner of a great rock, so that on three sides it was quite impregnable, and great windows were placed here where sling, or bow, or culverin could not reach, and consequently light and comfort, impossible to a position which had to be guarded, were secured. To the west was a great valley, and then, rising far away, great jagged mountain fastnesses, rising peak on peak, the sheer rock studded with mountain ash and thorn, whose roots clung in cracks and crevices and crannies of the stone. This was evidently the portion of the castle occupied in bygone days, for the furniture had more air of comfort than any I had seen. The windows were curtainless, and the yellow moonlight, flooding in through the diamond panes, enabled one to see even colours, whilst it softened the wealth of dust which lay over all and disguised in some measure the ravages of time and the moth. My lamp seemed to be of little effect in the brilliant moonlight, but I was glad to have it with me, for there was a dread loneliness in the place which chilled my heart and made my nerves tremble. Still, it was better than living alone in the rooms which I had come to hate from the presence of the Count, and after trying a little to school my nerves, I found a soft quietude come over me. Here I am, sitting at a little oak table where in old times possibly some fair lady sat to pen, with much thought and many blushes, her ill-spelt love-letter, and writing in my diary in shorthand all that has happened since I closed it last. It is nineteenth century up-to-date with a vengeance. And yet, unless my senses deceive me, the old centuries had, and have, powers of their own which mere 'modernity' cannot kill.

Later; The Morning of 16 May. – God preserve my sanity, for to this I am reduced. Safety and the assurance of safety are things of the past. Whilst I live on here there is but one thing to hope for: that I may not go mad, if, indeed, I be not mad already. If I be sane, then surely it is maddening to think that of all the foul things that lurk in this hateful place the Count is the least dreadful to me; that to him alone I can look for safety, even though this be only whilst I can serve his purpose. Great God! merciful God! Let me be calm, for out of that way lies madness indeed. I begin to get new lights on certain things which have puzzled me. Up to now I never quite knew what Shakespeare meant when he made Hamlet say: –

'My tablets! quick, my tablets!
'Tis meet that I put it down,' etc.,

for now, feeling as though my own brain were unhinged or as if the shock had come which must end in its undoing, I turn to my diary for repose. The habit of entering accurately must help to soothe me.

The Count's mysterious warning frightened me at the time; it frightens me more now when I think of it, for in future he has a fearful hold upon me. I shall fear to doubt what he may say!

When I had written in my diary and had fortunately replaced the book and pen in my pocket, I felt sleepy.

The Count's warning came into my mind, but I took a pleasure in disobeying it. The sense of sleep was upon me, and with it the obstinacy which sleep brings as outrider. The soft moonlight soothed, and the wide expanse without gave a sense of freedom which refreshed me. I determined not to return to-night to the gloom-haunted rooms, but to sleep here, where of old ladies had sat and sung and lived sweet lives whilst their gentle breasts were sad for their menfolk away in the midst of remorseless wars. I drew a great couch out of its place near the corner, so that, as I lay, I could look at the lovely view to east and south, and unthinking of and uncaring for the dust, composed myself for sleep.

I suppose I must have fallen asleep; I hope so, but I fear, for all that followed was startlingly real – so real that now, sitting here in the broad, full sunlight of the morning, I cannot in the least believe that it was all sleep.

I was not alone. The room was the same, unchanged in any way since I came into it; I could see along the floor, in the brilliant moonlight, my own footsteps marked where I had disturbed the long accumulation of dust. In the moonlight opposite me were three young women, ladies by their dress and manner. I thought at the time that I must be dreaming when I saw them, for, though the moonlight was behind them, they threw no shadow on the floor. They came close to me and looked at me for some time and then whispered together. Two were dark, and had high aquiline noses, like the Count's, and great dark, piercing eyes, that seemed to be almost red when contrasted with the pale yellow moon. The other was fair, as fair as can be, with great, wavy masses of golden hair and eyes like pale sapphires. I seemed somehow to know her face, and to know it in connection with some dreamy fear, but I could not recollect at the moment how or where. All three had brilliant white teeth, that shone like pearls against the ruby of their voluptuous lips. There was something about them that made me uneasy, some longing and at the same time some deadly fear. I felt in my heart a wicked, burning desire that they would kiss me with those red lips. It is not good to note this down, lest some day it should meet Mina's eyes and cause her pain; but it is the truth. They whispered together, and then they all three laughed – such a silvery, musical laugh, but as hard as though the sound never could have come through the softness of human lips. It was like the intolerable, tingling sweetness of water-glasses when played on by a cunning hand. The fair girl shook her head coquettishly, and the other two urged her on. One said: –

'Go on! You are first, and we shall follow; yours is the right to begin.' The other added: –

'He is young and strong; there are kisses for us all.' I lay quiet, looking out under my eyelashes in an agony of delightful anticipation. The fair girl advanced and bent over me till I could feel the movement of her breath upon me. Sweet it was in one sense, honey-sweet, and sent the same tingling through the nerves as her voice, but with a bitter underlying the sweet, a bitter offensiveness, as one smells in blood.

I was afraid to raise my eyelids, but looked out and saw perfectly under the lashes.

The fair girl went on her knees and bent over me, fairly gloating. There was a deliberate voluptuousness which was both thrilling and repulsive, and as she arched her neck she actually licked her lips like an animal, till I could see in the moonlight the moisture shining on the scarlet lips and on the red tongue as it lapped the white sharp teeth. Lower and lower went her head as the lips went below the range of my mouth and chin and seemed about to fasten on my throat. Then she paused, and I could hear the churning sound of her tongue as it licked her teeth and lips, and could feel the hot breath on my neck. Then the skin of my throat began to tingle as one's flesh does when the hand that is to tickle it approaches nearer – nearer. I could feel the soft, shivering touch of the lips on the supersensitive skin of my throat, and the hard dents of two sharp teeth, just touching and pausing there. I closed my eyes in a languorous ecstasy and waited – waited with beating heart.

But at that instant another sensation swept through me as quick as lightning. I was conscious of the presence of the Count, and of his being as if lapped in a storm of fury. As my eyes opened involuntarily I saw his strong hand grasp the slender neck of the fair woman and with giant's power draw it back, the blue eyes transformed with fury, the white teeth champing with rage, and the fair cheeks blazing red with passion. But the Count! Never did I imagine such wrath and fury, even in the demons of the pit. His eyes were positively blazing. The red light in them was lurid, as if the flames of hell-fire blazed behind them. His face was deathly pale, and the lines of it were hard like drawn wires; the thick eyebrows that met over the nose now seemed like a heaving bar of white-hot metal. With a fierce sweep of his arm, he hurled the woman from him, and then motioned to the others, as though he were beating them back; it was the same imperious gesture that I had seen used to the wolves. In a voice which, though low and almost a whisper, seemed to cut through the air and then ring round the room, he exclaimed: –

'How dare you touch him, any of you? How dare you cast eyes on him when I had forbidden it? Back, I tell you all! This man belongs to me! Beware how you meddle with him, or you'll have to deal with me.' The fair girl, with a laugh of ribald coquetry, turned to answer him: –

'You yourself never loved; you never love!' On this the other women joined, and such a mirthless, hard, soulless laughter rang through the room that it almost made me faint to hear; it seemed like the pleasure of fiends. Then the Count turned, after looking at my face attentively, and said in a soft whisper: –

'Yes, I too can love; you yourselves can tell it from the past. Is it not so? Well, now I promise you that when I am done with him, you shall kiss him at your will. Now go! go! I must awaken him, for there is work to be done.'

'Are we to have nothing to-night?' said one of them, with a low laugh, as she pointed to the bag which he had thrown upon the floor, and which moved as though there were some living thing within it. For answer he nodded his head. One of the women jumped forward and opened it. If my ears did not deceive me there was a gasp and a low wail, as of a half-smothered child. The women closed round, whilst I was aghast with horror; but as I looked they disappeared, and with them the dreadful bag. There was no door near them, and they could not have passed me without my noticing. They simply seemed to fade into the rays of the moonlight and pass out through the window, for I could see outside the dim, shadowy forms for a moment before they entirely faded away.

Then the horror overcame me, and I sank down unconscious.

The Furnished Room
O. Henry

*O. Henry was born William Sydney Porter to a North Carolina
family in 1862. As a young man he had various employment, including
the inauguration of a magazine, Rolling Stone, which failed, before
joining a bank. Accused of embezzlement, he fled America but
returned due to his wife's ill health. After her death he was imprisoned
for five years. Despite a struggle against alcoholism and impecunious
circumstances, he found fame, in New York, as a short story writer.
He died in 1910.*

Restless, shifting, fugacious as time itself, is a certain vast bulk of the population of the red-brick district of the lower West Side. Homeless, they have a hundred homes. They flit from furnished room to furnished room, transients for ever – transients in abode, transients in heart and mind. They sing 'Home Sweet Home' in ragtime; they carry their *lares et penates* in a bandbox; their vine is entwined about a picture hat; a rubber plant is their fig tree.

Hence the houses of this district, having had a thousand dwellers, should have a thousand tales to tell mostly dull ones, no doubt; but it would be strange if there could not be found a ghost or two in the wake of all these vagrant ghosts.

One evening after dark a young man prowled among these crumbling red mansions, ringing their bells. At the twelfth he rested his lean hand-baggage upon the step and wiped the dust from his hat-band and forehead. The bell sounded faint and far away in some remote, hollow depths.

To the door of this, the twelfth house whose bell he had rung, came a housekeeper who made him think of an unwholesome, surfeited worm that had eaten its nut to a hollow shell and now sought to fill the vacancy with edible lodgers.

He asked if there was a room to let.

'Come in,' said the housekeeper. Her voice came from her throat; her throat seemed lined with fur. 'I have the third floor back, vacant since a week back. Should you wish to look at it?'

The young man followed her up the stairs. A faint light from no particular source mitigated the shadows of the halls. They trod noiselessly upon a stair carpet that its own loom would have forsworn. It seemed to have become vegetable; to have degenerated in that rank, sunless air to lush lichen or spreading moss that grew in patches to the staircase and was viscid under the foot like organic matter. At each turn of the stairs were vacant niches in the wall. Perhaps plants had once been set within them. If so they had died in that foul and tainted air. It may be that statues of the saints had stood there, but it was not difficult to conceive that imps and devils had dragged them forth in the darkness and down to the unholy depths of some furnished pit below.

'This is the room,' said the housekeeper, from her furry throat. 'It's a nice room. It ain't often vacant. I had some most elegant people in it last summer – no trouble at all, and paid in advance to the minute. The water's at the end of the hall. Sprowls and Mooney kept it three months. They done a vaudeville sketch.

Miss B'retta Sprowls – you may have heard of her – Oh, that was just the stage names – right there over the dresser is where the marriage certificate hung, framed. The gas is here, and you see there is plenty of closet room. It's a room everybody likes. It never stays idle long.'

'Do you have many theatrical people rooming here?' asked the young man.

'They comes and goes. A good proportion of my lodgers is connected with the theatres. Yes, sir, this is the theatrical district. Actor people never stays long anywhere. I get my share. Yes, they comes and they goes.'

He engaged the room, paying for a week in advance. He was tired, he said, and would take possession at once. He counted out the money. The room had been made ready, she said, even to towels and water. As the housekeeper moved away he put, for the thousandth time, the question that he carried at the end of his tongue.

'A young girl – Miss Vashner – Miss Eloise Vashner – do you remember such a one among your lodgers? She would be singing on the stage, most likely. A fair girl, of medium height and slender, with reddish gold hair and a dark mole near her left eyebrow.'

'No, I don't remember the name. Them stage people has names they change as often as their rooms. They comes and they goes. No, I don't call that one to mind.'

No. Always no. Five months of ceaseless interrogation and the inevitable negative. So much time spent by day in questioning managers, agents, schools and choruses; by night among the audiences of theatres from all-star casts down to music-halls so low that he dreaded to find what he most hoped for. He who had loved her best had tried to find her. He was sure that since her disappearance from home this great water-girt city held her somewhere, but it was like a monstrous quicksand, shifting its particles constantly, with no foundation, its upper granules of to-day buried to-morrow in ooze and slime.

The furnished room received its latest guest with a first glow of pseudo-hospitality, a hectic, haggard, perfunctory welcome like the specious smile of a demirep. The sophistical comfort came in reflected gleams from the decayed furniture, the ragged brocade upholstery of a couch and two chairs, a footwide cheap pier glass between the two windows, from one or two gilt picture frames and a brass bedstead in a corner.

The guest reclined, inert, upon a chair, while the room, confused in speech as though it were an apartment in Babel, tried to discourse to him of its divers tenantry.

A polychromatic rug like some brilliant-flowered, rectangular, tropical islet lay surrounded by a billowy sea of soiled matting. Upon the gay-papered wall were those pictures that pursue the homeless one from house to house – The Huguenot Lovers, The First Quarrel, The Wedding Breakfast, Psyche at the Fountain. The mantel's chastely severe outline was ingloriously veiled behind some pert drapery drawn rakishly askew like the sashes of the Amazonian ballet. Upon it was some desolate flotsam cast aside by the room and marooned when a lucky sail had borne them to a fresh port – a trifling vase or two, pictures of actresses, a medicine bottle, some stray cards out of a deck.

One by one, as the characters of a cryptograph become explicit, the little signs left by the furnished room's procession of guests developed a significance. The threadbare space in the rug in front of the dresser told that lovely women had marched in the throng. Tiny finger-prints on the wall spoke of little prisoners trying to feel their way to sun and air. A splattered stain, raying like the shadow of a bursting bomb, witnessed where a hurled glass or bottle had splintered with its contents against the wall. Across the pier glass had been scrawled with a diamond in staggering letters the name 'Marie'. It seemed that the succession of dwellers in the furnished room had turned in fury – perhaps tempted beyond forbearance by its garish coldness – and wreaked upon it their passions. The furniture was chipped and bruised; the couch, distorted by bursting springs, seemed a horrible monster that had been slain during the stress of some grotesque convulsion. Some more potent up-heaval had cloven a great slice from the marble mantel. Each plank in the floor owned its particular cant and shriek as from a separate and individual agony. It seemed incredible that all this malice and injury had been wrought upon the room by those who had called it for a time their home; and yet it may have been the cheated home instinct surviving blindly, the resentful rage at false household gods that had kindled their wrath. A hut that is our own we can sweep and adorn and cherish.

The young tenant in the chair allowed these thoughts to file, soft-shod, through his mind, while there drifted into the room furnished sounds and furnished scents. He heard in one room a tittering and incontinent, slack laughter; in others the monologue of a scold, the rattling of dice, a lullaby, and one crying dully; above him a banjo tinkled with spirit. Doors banged somewhere; the elevated trains roared intermittently; a cat yowled miserably upon a back fence. And he breathed the breath of the house – a dank savour rather than a smell –

a cold, musty effluvium as from underground vaults mingled with the reeking exhalations of linoleum and mildewed and rotten woodwork.

Then, suddenly, as he rested there, the room was filled with the strong, sweet odour of mignonette. It came as upon a single buffet of wind with such sureness and fragrance and emphasis that it almost seemed a living visitant. And the man cried aloud, 'What, dear?' as if he had been called, and sprang up and faced about. The rich odour clung to him and wrapped him about. He reached out his arms for it, all his senses for the time confused and commingled. How could one be peremptorily called by an odour? Surely it must have been a sound. But, was it not the sound that had touched, that had caressed him?

'She has been in this room,' he cried, and he sprang to wrest from it a token, for he knew he would recognize the smallest thing that had belonged to her or that she had touched. This enveloping scent of mignonette, the odour that she had loved and made her own – whence came it?

The room had been but carelessly set in order. Scattered upon the flimsy dresser scarf were half a dozen hairpins – those discreet, indistinguishable friends of womankind, feminine of gender, infinite of mood and uncommunicative of tense. These he ignored, conscious of their triumphant lack of identity. Ransacking the drawers of the dresser he came upon a discarded, tiny, ragged handkerchief. He pressed it to his face. It was racy and insolent with heliotrope; he hurled it to the floor. In another drawer he found odd buttons, a theatre programme, a pawnbroker's card, two lost marshmallows, a book on the divination of dreams. In the last was a woman's black satin hair-bow, which halted him, poised between ice and fire. But the black satin hair-bow also is femininity's demure, impersonal, common ornament, and tells no tales.

And then he traversed the room like a hound on the scent, skimming the walls, considering the corners of the bulging matting on his hands and knees, rummaging mantel and tables, the curtains and hangings, the drunken cabinet in the corner, for a visible sign unable to perceive that she was there beside, around, against, within, above him, clinging to him, wooing him, calling him so poignantly through the finer senses that even his grosser ones became cognizant of the call. Once again he answered loudly, 'Yes, dear!' and turned, wild-eyed, to gaze on vacancy, for he could not yet discern form and colour and love and outstretched arms in the odour of mignonette. Oh, God! whence that odour, and since when have odours had a voice to call? Thus he groped.

He burrowed in crevices and corners, and found corks and cigarettes. These he passed in passive contempt. But once he found in a fold of the matting a half-smoked cigar, and this he ground beneath his heel with a green and trenchant oath. He sifted the room from end to end. He found dreary and ignoble small records of many a peripatetic tenant; but of her whom he sought, and who may have lodged there, and whose spirit seemed to hover there, he found no trace.

And then he thought of the housekeeper.

He ran from the haunted room downstairs and to a door that showed a crack of light. She came out to his knock. He smothered his excitement as best he could.

'Will you tell me, madam,' he besought her, 'who occupied the room I have before I came?'

'Yes, sir. I can tell you again. 'Twas Sprowls and Mooney, as I said. Miss B'retta Sprowls it was in the theatres, but Missis Mooney she was. My house is well known for respectability. The marriage certificate hung, framed, on a nail over ——'

'What kind of a lady was Miss Sprowls – in looks, I mean?'

'Why, black-haired, sir, short and stout, with a comical face. They left a week ago Tuesday.'

'And before they occupied it?'

'Why, there was a single gentleman connected with the draying business. He left owing me a week. Before him was Missis Crowder and her two children, that stayed four months; and back of them was old Mr. Doyle, whose sons paid for him. He kept the room six months. That goes back a year, sir, and further I do not remember.'

He thanked her and crept back to his room. The room was dead. The essence that had vivified it was gone. The perfume of mignonette had departed. In its place was the old, stale odour of mouldy house furniture, of atmosphere in storage.

The ebbing of his hope drained his faith. He sat staring at the yellow, singing gaslight. Soon he walked to the bed and began to tear the sheets into strips. With the blade of his knife he drove them tightly into every crevice around windows and door. When all was snug and taut he turned out the light, turned the gas full on again and laid himself gratefully upon the bed.

*   *   *

It was Mrs. McCool's night to go with the can for beer. So she fetched it and sat with Mrs. Purdy in one of those subterranean retreats where housekeepers foregather and the worm dieth seldom.

'I rented out my third floor back, this evening,' said Mrs. Purdy, across a fine circle of foam. 'A young man took it. He went up to bed two hours ago.'

'Now, did ye, Mrs. Purdy, ma'am?' said Mrs. McCool, with intense admiration. 'You do be a wonder for rentin' rooms of that kind. And did ye tell him, then?' she concluded in a husky whisper, laden with mystery.

'Rooms,' said Mrs. Purdy, in her furriest tones, 'are furnished for to rent. I did not tell him, Mrs. McCool.'

' 'Tis right ye are, ma'am; 'tis by renting rooms we kape alive. Ye have the rale sense for business, ma'am. There be many people will rayjict the rentin' of a room if they be tould a suicide has been after dyin' in the bed of it.'

'As you say, we has our living to be making,' remarked Mrs. Purdy.

'Yis, ma'am; 'tis true. 'Tis just one wake ago this day I helped ye lay out the third floor back. A pretty slip of a colleen she was to be killin' herself wid the gas – a swate little face she had, Mrs. Purdy, ma'am.'

'She'd a-been called handsome, as you say,' said Mrs. Purdy, assenting but critical, 'but for that mole she had a-growin' by her left eyebrow. Do fill up your glass again, Mrs. McCool.'

The Forsaken of God
William Mudford

Mudford was born in London in 1782 and devoted most of his life to journalism and writing. He was a conservative, an admirer of Burke, and a friend of Canning, the Prime Minister. For a period, Mudford edited the 'Courier,' an evening newspaper that rivalled 'The Times.' Such was his popularity that when he left the 'Courier,' it went into decline, and eventually ceased publication. Due to economic problems, he later assumed editorship of the 'Kentish Observer.' He died in 1848.

'For Heaven's sake! Frederick, do not go,' exclaimed the terrified Adolphine, holding her brother by the arm to detain him.

'Why not?' replied Frederick. 'If Hermann can do *his* part, I'll be sworn to go through mine.'

' 'Tis unholy! 'tis hellish! 'tis an impious daring of the Almighty! and you shall *not* go,' said Adolphine. 'My blood curdles at my heart to *think* only of what you have said!'

'Why, look you, Adolphine,' answered Frederick, laughing, as he disengaged himself gently from the clinging arms of his sister; 'what is it after all? Hermann says he can raise the dead; and I say, if he can, I am he that will hold a parley with the dead; a conference such as living man ne'er yet had.'

'Oh, God!' exclaimed Adolphine, covering her eyes with her hands, and shuddering as she spoke, 'the bare imagination of it is horrible.'

'Shall I tell you a secret?' continued Frederick. 'I believe Hermann less able to perform his part than I mine.'

'Still, it is sinful mockery – if it be only mockery,' said Adolphine.

The deep heavy bell of the cathedral struck eleven. Frederick starting up, threw his cloak round him, put on his hat, and prepared to quit the house.

'I have not a moment to play with now,' said he. 'Hermann expects me before twelve, and it is a long walk to where he lives.'

'Do not, do not go!' exclaimed Adolphine, in a tone of earnest supplication, as she once more flung herself upon his bosom to detain him.

'By my faith, but I must. If Hermann has spoken truly, he has ere this gone through pains and torments, to vex the graves which are to yield up their pale inhabitants for my pleasure, that I dare not trifle with. Besides, would he not ever after despise me as a coward, big of speech, but faint of resolution, should I leave to him the boast of having prepared a scene which I was too sick at heart to look upon? To-morrow, with the dawn, I shall return; and then, Adolphine –'

'And then, it will be time to tell her more, thou loitering babbler,' exclaimed a voice, whose freezing breath fell upon the ear of Frederick like an icy current of keen winter air. He alone heard it. He started and shivered at the mysterious rebuke. The next moment he was on his way to Hermann's dwelling in the mountains, and Adolphine was on her knees, praying fervently for his safety.

Hermann and Frederick were fellow students in one of the German universities. It matters little what one; as little, when the compact we are describing was made; whether a century or two centuries ago. It *was* made – for its history is extant. Hermann, who was older by some years than Frederick, was reputed to be deeply skilled in the lore of necromancy and magic, and to have acquired the fearful power of controlling the spirits of darkness, so as to make them work his will. Whether he really possessed this power, no one knew, though every one asserted it, and Hermann himself did not deny it.

It chanced on one occasion, when he and Frederick were walking through a churchyard, the latter, who delighted in strange, wild fancies, observed, as he paused to survey the tombs around them, 'If a man now could bid these graves yawn, and cast forth their dead, to be questioned of what they once were, and what they are, and they constrained to answer truly whatsoever might be demanded of them – God of Heaven! what marvellous secrets we should learn!'

'As how?' inquired Hermann.

'Oh! think ye not that we should find innocence that had bled upon the scaffold, for unacted crimes? Murder, and sacrilege, and robbery, and sin of every kind, dying on beds of down, cozening to the last all but Heaven and a howling conscience? Should we not see hearts broken by secret griefs, that never were told to mortal ears? Fathers and mothers killed by their unnatural children? – the young and beautiful withered by love's perjuries? poison and steel shortening the years that lay between heirs and their inheritance? And all these undiscovered villainies smuggled out of the world, with certificates of old age – consumption – apoplexy – from grave physicians who take fees to give names to what they cannot cure.'

Hermann mused in silence.

'Here,' continued Frederick, planting his foot upon a new-made grave – 'here lies one who but yesterday was laid in the earth perhaps. Imagine I could say to him or her arise – that I could call back speech and memory to the dull clod – that I could hold in my hand, as a book, the heart that has ceased to throb. Should I not read there something which the world had never read, during all the long years it dwelt in it?'

' 'Tis an odd fancy, Frederick,' exclaimed Hermann; 'a very odd fancy. Since when has such a notion possessed you?'

'Since my mother died,' replied Frederick emphatically.

'And she died –'

'Oh, ask the doctor. He'll tell you 'twas of atrophy, and prove it by his art. I laughed amid my tears to hear them talk; and then it was I first thought how the dead would answer for themselves.'

'Let us go,' said Hermann, and they quitted the churchyard.

Many times afterwards the two friends discoursed upon this theme, which Hermann could not banish from his thoughts; and one evening, when they were passing through this same churchyard, he thus addressed Frederick:

'Do you remember,' said he, 'our conversation here, some months ago?'

'I do; and our frequent ones since.'

'*I* can perform the thing you wish.'

'Would you were able!' answered Frederick.

'I can do it.'

'What?'

'Lay open these graves!'

'Pooh!' exclaimed Frederick laughing. 'Come along, Hermann; you are making sport of me.'

'Hear me,' said Hermann, remaining fixed to the spot where he stood. 'I am not, as you imagine, merrily disposed; but I mean to use no persuasion – no argument with you. Simply, and in plain words, I repeat, I can lay these graves open, and command the dust and ashes they contain to take forms of life: even the very shapes they bore when living.'

'Thou canst do this?'

'This, and more. They shall reveal to you those marvellous secrets you spoke of.'

'Hermann!' exclaimed Frederick, looking at his friend with an eye that flashed horrible delight. 'Hermann! swear that you will do this; swear, by some oath, terrible as the thing itself, and I will pawn my soul to the eternal enemy of man for the pledge of my part in it.'

'There needs nor oath nor plight to bind the willing and the bold. I am the first; are *you* the second?'

'Here is my hand. When shall it be?' replied Frederick.

'We will settle that as we walk along,' answered Hermann.

They did settle it; and the night was now come in which Frederick was to be convinced (for he doubted to the last) whether Hermann could really perform this fearful feat of sorcery. He arrived at his house later than the time appointed, in consequence of the delay occasioned by Adolphine's entreaties to forgo the meeting altogether; and Hermann was looking out for him. He returned to his room, followed by Frederick.

'I had worked for nothing,' said he, angrily, 'had I not gone beyond the need of this night's labour, to break the spell of a fond girl. Are these matters that women should know? Adolphine is on her knees still, and her prayers have a holiness in them that thwarts and disturbs my purpose. But I can perform – I can perform!' he muttered to himself as he rolled something in the palms of his hands that emitted sparks of a crimson hue, with a loud crackling. 'I can – ha! bravely! bravely!' and he increased the rolling motion of his hands; 'her eyes close – her head droops – 'tis a sound sleep: it will last till the lark sings.'

As he uttered these words, his hands unclosed; the palms were of a deep, blood-red colour, but there was no visible appearance of any substance that had been rubbed between them.

Frederick remembered the freezing voice that had rebuked him, and no longer doubted of Hermann's power. If he could thus hold communion with the living, why might not the dead be subject to his art?

The room was lighted by a single taper, which burned thick and duskily. On a table in the middle of it lay several open books, traced with strange characters, and encircled with the skeletons of birds, reptiles, and animals. The appearance of Hermann himself was so strangely altered that Frederick could scarcely recognise him. His face was pallid even to ghastliness; his arms were naked to the elbow; his long black hair knotted; and his tall gaunt figure enveloped in a robe made from the skin of a leopard. The girdle by which it was fastened looked like twisted snakes, for there was a constant heaving and writhing of it about his body.

Frederick noted these things while Hermann was speaking. When he ceased, he said, with an air of gaiety,

'I like your dress vastly, Hermann; 'tis excellent masquerade; but am not I too, to be equipped for this great occasion?'

'*There* hangs thy robe,' replied Hermann, pointing with his finger.

Frederick started. Was it Hermann that had spoken? or was it a voice creaked from the bony lungs of death himself? He turned round in the direction of the pointed finger. Again he started recoiling several paces. – An arm – an arm merely – joined to no body, was extended behind him, holding a winding sheet. The flesh was upon it, but livid and in corruption: and there it hung, suspended in mid air, balanced and supported he knew not how, offering him a shroud that had the soil of the grave upon it!

'There needs nor oath nor plight to bind the willing and the bold,' said Hermann, in the same unearthly tone. 'I am the first: art thou the second?'

'Ay!' responded Frederick; 'thou hast my word, Hermann; but –'

''Tis past questioning now,' interrupted Hermann. 'The dead are waiting for us, and we *must* go. Quick, quick; clothe thyself.'

Frederick rallied from his trepidation, and advancing with a resolute step, plucked the winding sheet from the spectre hand. At the same moment there was heard a low wailing sound, which continued till he had folded round his creeping flesh the sepulchral garment.

The horrible half-decayed arm remained. Hermann drew from his bosom a charmed glove, woven of the down that lines the screech-owl's wings. He gave it to Frederick.

'*That* must with us,' said he, pointing to the arm; 'but at the touch of living flesh it would dissolve to putrid jelly. Put on this; grasp it boldly; and all is done till we stand in the churchyard.'

Frederick did as he was commanded without uttering a word. He put on the charmed glove; he grasped the arm. It had substance; it was heavy; and so chilling cold that it benumbed his own, as if it were solid ice. His teeth chattered; his body shook; the shroud struck a freezing shudder through his veins; and this seemed to heighten it. He looked at Hermann. He would have spoken, but his lips were rigid; as unapt for motion as the marble lips of a statue.

'From this moment until sunrise,' said Hermann, 'you have no power to exchange thoughts but with the dead. You hunger for their secrets; but know you not that the grave is a curtain dropped between two worlds? He who uplifts it, cannot be of both, save at the price you have to pay. Come!'

Frederick heard this terrible denunciation with an appalled spirit. He determined to renounce his design.

He strove to fling the arm from him. – It clung to his hand, as if it had been riveted there with clasps of iron. He endeavoured to tear off the shroud. It seemed to have grown to him; and that it would have been as easy to wrench away his limbs.

Hermann laughed aloud as he repeated Frederick's own words: 'Swear that you will do this – swear by some oath terrible as the thing itself, and I will pawn my soul to the eternal enemy of man for the pledge of my part in it!' – 'Saidst thou not so? And dost thou quail already? Summon all that's man in thee for what remains. Come! They who wait for us will grow impatient.'

Hermann led the way; Frederick followed with a staggering step. The night was preternaturally dark; it appeared as if they were walking under a thick canopy of black mist, which veiled the heavens from their sight. The path that Hermann took was through the tangled alleys of the forest; a nearer, but more difficult road to the churchyard. He talked, sung, laughed, and acted, the whole way the part of a man whose spirits were elated by the prospect of a festal meeting. He jeered Frederick ironically upon what he called, 'his dogged silence': the forest rang with his laughter at every stumble he made; and he bade him note how nimbly he threaded the narrow paths, though he had nor more nor better eyes then himself. Frederick listened to him with feelings which it were impossible to describe. It was not Hermann he was following – he was sure it was not Hermann – it was some fiend, in Hermann's shape, for Hermann was grave, austere, melancholy – never given to gamesome moods; and least of all could Hermann, his friend, his brother almost, exult so *like* a fiend in the agony of mind he was enduring.

*   *   *

They stand beside a grave. Hermann sprinkles upon it a powder, which falls in sparkles of light from his fingers. The earth begins to heave; and presently, as a volcano casts up its ashes, the grave empties itself. Slowly and slowly, like the rippling waves of a becalmed ocean, it rises to the surface, divides, and falls in crumbling heaps on either side. Then there ascends the venerable figure of an aged man, clothed in robes of purple and scarlet, the ensigns of senatorial dignity. At the same moment, the spectre arm, by wondrous motion of its own, tears itself aloft, and becomes a dimly gleaming torch; each livid finger sending forth pale red dusky flames, which fling a horrid glare upon the cadaverous features of the phantom.

'I cannot hold him longer than while thy quickened pulse shall beat a hundred,' said Hermann in a whisper. 'In that space thou must master what secrets thou would'st learn.'

'I know thee!' exclaimed Frederick, with a faltering voice, 'thou wert the traitor, Wulfstein, who conspired against thy prince's life! I saw the headsman execute justice on thee, thou, to the last, calling Heaven to witness thy innocence: but all men knew thee guilty.'

'*One* man knew I was not,' said the phantom; and a grim smile grew upon his corpse-like face.

'And he – ,' rejoined Frederick.

'Shall I name him?'

'Aye – '

' 'TWAS THY FATHER! Most foully he shed *my* blood to save his own!'

The phantom vanished – the grave closed – the pale-red dusky flames of the unhallowed torch expired – a yell of exulting voices, as if the fiends of the abyss were triumphing, sounded in the air – and Frederick was again mute. Hermann clapped him on the shoulder, exclaiming, in a tone of taunting bitterness, 'Rare secrets! brave secrets! marvellous revelations for the living!'

*   *   *

They stand beside a second grave. The same ceremonies – the same effects: the earth heaves, the sepulchre yawns, the torch of the charnel-house uprears itself, and burns. The resemblance of a fair beautiful youth, with radiant eyes and clustering locks, stands before them.

'I know *thee*, too!' exclaimed Frederick striving in vain to draw down his arm, so that the lurid flame might not gleam upon the shape – 'My brother!'

'Who died by a brother's hand!'

'But I was guiltless – I was guiltless, dear Francis!' rejoined Frederick, in a tone of piercing anguish. 'My

arrow flew at the fierce wolf, when thou, crossing its path, received it in thy heart!'

'Did I upbraid thee for my death, as that heart's blood fell upon thee? Were not my words words of consolation? Strove I not to soothe the pangs with which that blameless deed of slaughter filled thee?'

'Thou didst – thou didst! Avaunt! Hide thee from mine eyes, or I shall grow mad. Oh! I sought not *this*!'

'Think of the wretched misery our mother bore, whilst thou whole days and nights didst suffer her to mourn, in ignorance, my loss! Think what a stain, even to this hour, lies upon the innocent name of one who lives dishonoured in the suspicion of *thy* act! Thou canst not redeem the past: but thou mayst make the future witness of thy tardy justice.'

Frederick had covered his eyes with his hand, unable to look upon this vision. When he withdrew his hand it was gone. They were again in silence and darkness; but he heard the voice of Hermann at his side, in the same tone of taunting bitterness, repeating his own words: 'Thou saidst truly, my friend. Thou hast now "read something, which the world never read". Oh, these dead! "how they answer for themselves", Frederick! 'Tis rare sport to bid them thus arise – to "call back speech and memory to the dull clods" – to "hold their hearts in our hands, and peruse them as a book!" Truth is not of this world; and they were fools who looked for her in the bottom of a well; her temple is the grave! her oracles, dust and ashes!'

*   *   *

The scene was changed. They stood beneath the ruined porch of the church. The doors flew open with a rattling sound; they entered: the vast edifice was wrapped in impenetrable gloom, except the little circle of dismal light from the horrible torch. They advanced to the altar, the steps of which Hermann ascended alone, silently motioning his companion to remain. He waved his hands over the tall wax tapers that stood upon the table of the altar, when, by some strange spell, blue forked flames descended upon them, and they burned with dim ghastly flashes that shot forth each moment. By this fitful glare Frederick could perceive all he did and all he looked; for this aspect was now wild, terrific, demon-like.

He took the sacramental chalice, and stretching forth his bare arm, cried in a loud voice, 'Come ye viewless ministers of this dread hour! come from the fenny lake, the hanging rock, and the midnight cave! The moon is red – the stars are out – the sky is burning – and all nature stands aghast at what we do!' Then replacing the sacred vessel on the altar, he drew, one by one, from different parts of his body, from his knotted hair, from his bosom, from beneath his nails, the unholy things which he cast into it.

'This,' said he, ' I plucked from the beak of a raven feeding on a murderer's brains! This is the mad dog's foam! These the spurgings of a dead man's eyes, gathered since the rising of the evening star! This is a screech-owl's egg! This a single drop of black blood, squeezed from the heart of a sweltered toad! This, an adder's tongue! And here, ten grains of the gray moss that grew upon a skull which had lain in the charnel-house three hundred years! What! not yet?' And his eyes seemed like balls of fire as he cast them upwards. 'Not yet? I call ye once! I call ye twice! Dare ye deny me! Nay, then, as I call ye thrice, I'll wound mine arm, and as it drops, I'll breathe a spell shall cleave the ground and drag you here!'

He held his left arm over the chalice, clutched it with his hand, and as if the talons of an eagle had infixed themselves, the blood spouted forth. While it dripped into the vessel he gasped for breath like a strong man fighting hard with his last agonies.

Suddenly the tapers were extinguished, and there remained only the fearful glare that flickered horribly from the unhallowed torch. It reached not to the altar; so Frederick saw not Hermann. But he saw upon its lowest step – HIS MOTHER! even as he had seen her the day he returned without his brother, when he spoke not the word that would have spared those long hours of grief which the mystery of his absence caused; to be followed, at last, by all a mother's heart could feel for the untimely death of a beloved son. He bent his knee in reverential awe before the sacred shade; and his soul grew faint within him; for there was upon that maternal face a sad look of pity and of wrath. He had thoughts that burned for utterance, but he had no tongue to give them utterance. The form spoke:

'Why hast thou troubled me in death, my son? Why hast thou in life arrayed thee in that garb of death? Why has thou disturbed MY sepulchre, for the shroud that infolds thee?'

A shriek of horror burst from him, as again he strove, but vainly, to tear off the sacrilegious spoil of his mother's grave.

'Son, thou hast sought, unholily, the secrets of the dead; hear MINE! The canker that preyed upon my life, was grief for thee. The forsaken of God are they alone who forsake God. All sinners else may hope to be partakers of his infinite mercies. THOU WERT GOD-FORSAKEN! Thou clothedst thyself in the pride of thy under-standing – said there was NO GOD – and lived as if thou didst believe in thy impiety. I loved thee, for I bare thee – thou wert my child; but the thorns planted in my heart by the knowledge that my child must perish eternally, wounded it to death!'

The shadow faded away, and again the yell of exulting voices sounded in the ears of Frederick, as he lay prostrate on the cold damp pavement, shedding involuntary tears. They fell from his eyes like drops of molten lead. His brain seemed on fire. He groaned, and howled, and gnashed his teeth, and dashed his face furiously against the stones. He heard the voice of Hermann. Oh! the damning chuckle of that voice, as he jealously shouted – ' "Rare secrets! brave secrets! marvellous revelations for the living!" "Since when hath such a notion possessed you?" "Since my mother died!" "And she died – ?" "Oh ask the doctor," ha! ha! ha! "he'll tell you 'twas of atrophy;" ha! ha! ha! "I laughed amid my tears to hear them talk; and then it was that I first thought how the dead would answer for themselves." Ha! ha! ha! Laugh, man, laugh as I do! Laugh NOW, amid thy tears, thou desperate fool!'

The next morning, Frederick was found a corpse in the abbey church, at the foot of his mother's tomb, leading to the altar. Adolphine told what she knew of the compact between him and Hermann; but Hermann brought forward two fellow students with whom he had passed the preceding evening; and his own servant proved that he retired to bed at eleven, where he found him at the usual hour when he went to call him. Hermann himself, too, denied that he had ever entered into such a compact; wept for the death of his friend, and triumphed over his accusers. Yet, had he been required to bare his left arm, there would have appeared upon it the fresh blood marks of lacerated flesh, as if torn by an eagle's talons!

The Werewolf
Frederick Marryat

*Marryat was born in 1792. His father was a landowner and the chairman
of Lloyds. At fourteen he joined the navy and rose to the rank of captain.
He saw action in the Mediterranean, and was honoured for his conduct
in the Burmese War. He also devised a code for signalling with flags.
Marryat made full use of his experiences at sea in his novels. He was a
prolific writer, but is mainly remembered today for his children's stories.
He died in 1848.*

'My father was not born, or originally a resident in the Hartz Mountains; he was a serf of a Hungarian nobleman, of great possessions, in Transylvania; but although a serf, he was not by any means a poor or illiterate man. In fact, he was rich, and his intelligence and respectability were such, that he had been raised by his lord to the stewardship; but whoever may happen to be a born serf, a serf must he remain, even though he become a wealthy man: such was the condition of my father. My father had been married for about five years; and by his marriage had three children – my eldest brother Cæsar, myself (Hermann), and a sister named Marcella. You know, Philip, that Latin is still the language spoken in that country; and that will account for our high-sounding names. My mother was a very beautiful woman, unfortunately more beautiful than virtuous: she was seen and admired by the lord of the soil; my father was sent away upon some mission; and during his absence, my mother, flattered by the attentions and won by the assiduities of this nobleman, yielded to his wishes. It so happened that my father returned very unexpectedly, and discovered the intrigue. The evidence of my mother's shame was positive; he surprised her in the company of her seducer! Carried away by the impetuosity of his feelings, he watched the opportunity of a meeting taking place between them, and murdered both his wife and her seducer. Conscious that, as a serf, not even the provocation which he had received would be allowed as a justification of his conduct, he hastily collected together what money he could lay his hands upon, and, as we were then in the depths of winter, he put his horses to the sleigh, and taking his children with him, he set off in the middle of the night, and was far away before the tragical circumstance had transpired. Aware that he would be pursued, and that he had no chance of escape if he remained in any portion of his native country (in which the authorities could lay hold of him), he continued his flight without intermission until he had buried himself in the intricacies and seclusion of the Hartz Mountains. Of course, all that I have now told you I learned afterwards. My oldest recollections are knit to a rude, yet comfortable cottage, in which I lived with my father, brother, and sister. It was on the confines of one of those vast forests which cover the northern part of Germany; around it were a few acres of ground, which, during the summer months, my father cultivated, and which, though they yielded a doubtful harvest, were sufficient for our support. In the winter we remained much indoors, for, as my father followed the chase, we were left alone, and the wolves during that season incessantly prowled about. My father had purchased the cottage, and land about it, of one of the rude foresters, who gain their livelihood partly by hunting, and partly by burning charcoal, for the

purpose of smelting the ore from the neighbouring mines; it was distant about two miles from any other habitation. I can call to mind the whole landscape now; the tall pines which rose up on the mountain above us, and the wide expanse of the forest beneath, on the topmost boughs and heads of whose trees we looked down from our cottage as the mountain below us rapidly descended into the distant valley. In summer time the prospect was beautiful: but during the severe winter a more desolate scene could not well be imagined.

'I said that, in the winter, my father occupied himself with the chase; every day he left us, and often would he lock the door, that we might not leave the cottage. He had no one to assist him or to take care of us – indeed, it was not easy to find a female servant who would live in such a solitude; but, could he have found one, my father would not have received her, for he had imbibed a horror of the sex, as the difference of his

conduct towards us, his two boys, and my poor little sister Marcella evidently proved. You may suppose we were sadly neglected; indeed, we suffered much, for my father, fearful that we might come to some harm, would not allow us fuel when he left the cottage; and we were obliged, therefore, to creep under the heaps of bears' skins, and there to keep ourselves as warm as we could until he returned in the evening, when a blazing fire was our delight. That my father chose this restless sort of life may appear strange, but the fact was, that he could not remain quiet; whether from the remorse for having committed murder or from the misery consequent on his change of situation, or from both combined, he was never happy unless he was in a state of activity. Children, however, when left so much to themselves, acquire a thoughtfulness not common to their age. So it was with us; and during the short cold days of winter, we would sit silent, longing for the happy

hours when the snow would melt and the leaves burst out, and the birds begin their songs, and when we should again be set at liberty.

'Such was our peculiar and savage sort of life until my brother Cæsar was nine, myself seven, and my sister five years old, when the circumstances occurred on which is based the extraordinary narrative which I am about to relate.

'One evening my father returned home rather later than usual; he had been unsuccessful, and as the weather was very severe, and many feet of snow were upon the ground, he was not only very cold, but in a very bad humour. He had brought in wood, and we were all three gladly assisting each other in blowing on the embers to create a blaze, when he caught poor little Marcella by the arm and threw her aside; the child fell, struck her mouth, and bled very much. My brother ran to raise her up. Accustomed to ill-usage, and afraid of my father, she did not dare to cry, but looked up in his face very piteously. My father drew his stool nearer to the hearth, muttered something in abuse of women, and busied himself with the fire, which both my brother and I had deserted when our sister was so unkindly treated. A cheerful blaze was soon the result of his exertions; but we did not, as usual, crowd round it. Marcella, still bleeding, retired to a corner, and my brother and I took our seats beside her, while my father hung over the fire gloomily and alone. Such had been our position for about half an hour, when the howl of a wolf, close under the window of the cottage, fell on our ears. My father started up, and seized his gun; the howl was repeated; he examined the priming, and then hastily left the cottage, shutting the door after him. We all waited (anxiously listening), for we thought that if he succeeded in shooting the wolf, he would return in a better humour; and, although he was harsh to all of us, and particularly so to our little sister, still we loved our father, and loved to see him cheerful and happy, for what else had we to look up to? And I may here observe that perhaps there never were three children who were fonder of each other; we did not, like other children, fight and dispute together; and if, by chance, any disagreement did arise, between my elder brother and me, little Marcella would run to us, and kissing us both, seal, through her entreaties, the peace between us. Marcella was a lovely, amiable child; I can recall her beautiful features even now. Alas! poor little Marcella.

'We waited for some time, but the report of the gun did not reach us, and my elder brother then said, "Our father has followed the wolf, and will not be back for some time. Marcella, let us wash the blood from your mouth, and then we will leave this corner and go to the fire to warm ourselves."

'We did so, and remained there until near midnight, every minute wondering, as it grew later, why our father did not return. We had no idea that he was in any danger, but we thought that he must have chased the wolf for a very long time. "I will look out and see if father is coming," said my brother Cæsar, going to the door. "Take care," said Marcella, "the wolves must be about now, and we cannot kill them, brother." My brother opened the door very cautiously, and but a few inches; he peeped out. "I see nothing," said he, after a time, and once more he joined us at the fire. "We have had no supper," said I, for my father usually cooked the meat as soon as he came home; and during his absence we had nothing but the fragments of the preceding day.

' "And if our father comes home after his hunt, Cæsar," said Marcella, "he will be pleased to have some supper; let us cook it for him and for ourselves." Cæsar climbed upon the stool, and reached down some meat – I forget now whether it was venison or bear's meat, but we cut off the usual quantity, and proceeded to dress it, as we used to do under our father's superintendence. We were all busy putting it into the platters before the fire, to await his coming, when we heard the sound of a horn. We listened – there was a noise outside, and a minute afterwards my father entered, ushered in a young female, and a large dark man in a hunter's dress.

'Perhaps I had better now relate what was only known to me many years afterwards. When my father had left the cottage, he perceived a large white wolf about thirty yards from him; as soon as the animal saw my father, it retreated slowly growling and snarling. My father followed; the animal did not run, but always kept at some distance; and my father did not like to fire until he was pretty certain that his ball would take effect; thus they went on for some time, the wolf now leaving my father far behind, and then stopping and snarling defiance at him, and then, again, on his approach, setting off at speed.

'Anxious to shoot the animal (for the white wolf is very rare), my father continued the pursuit for several hours, during which he continually ascended the mountain.

'You must know, Philip, that there are peculiar spots on those mountains which are supposed, and, as my story will prove, truly supposed, to be inhabited by the evil influences: they are well known to the huntsmen, who invariably avoid them. Now, one of these spots, an open space in the pine forest above us, had been pointed out to my father as dangerous on that account. But whether he disbelieved these wild stories, or whether, in his eager pursuit of the chase, he disregarded them, I know not; certain, however, it is, that he was decoyed by the white wolf to this open space, when the animal appeared to slacken her speed. My father approached, came close up to her, raised his gun to his shoulder, and was about to fire, when the wolf suddenly disappeared. He thought that the snow on the ground must have dazzled his sight, and he let down his gun to look for the beast – but she was gone; how she could have escaped over the clearance, without his seeing her, was beyond his comprehension. Mortified at the ill-success of his chase, he was about to retrace his steps, when he heard the distant sound of a horn. Astonishment at such a sound – at such an hour – in such a wilderness, made him forget for the moment his disappointment, and he remained riveted to the spot. In a minute the horn was blown a second time, and at no great distance; my father stood still, and listened; a third time it was blown. I forget the term used to express it, but it was the signal which, my father well knew, implied that the party was lost in the woods. In a few minutes more my father beheld a man on horseback, with a female seated on the crupper, enter the cleared space, and ride up to him. At first, my father called to mind the strange stories which he had heard of the supernatural beings who were said to frequent these mountains; but the nearer approach of the parties satisfied him that they were mortals like himself. As soon as they came up to him, the man who guided the horse accosted him. "Friend hunter, you are out late, the better fortune for us; we have ridden far, and are in fear of our lives, which are eagerly sought after. These mountains have enabled us to elude our pursuers; but if we find not shelter and refreshment, that will avail us little, as we must perish from hunger and the inclemency of the night. My daughter, who rides behind me, is now more dead than alive – say, can you assist us in our difficulty?"

' "My cottage is some few miles distant," replied my father, "but I have little to offer you besides a shelter from the weather; to the little I have you are welcome. May I ask whence you come?"

' "Yes, friend, it is no secret now; we have escaped from Transylvania, where my daughter's honour and my life were equally in jeopardy!"

'This information was quite enough to raise an interest in my father's heart. He remembered his own escape: he remembered the loss of his wife's honour, and the tragedy by which it was wound up. He immediately, and warmly, offered all the assistance which he could afford them.

' "There is no time to be lost then, good sir," observed the horseman; "my daughter is chilled with the frost, and cannot hold out much longer against the severity of the weather."

' "Follow me," replied my father, leading the way towards his home.

' "I was lured away in pursuit of a large white wolf," observed my father; "it came to the very window of my hut, or I should not have been out at this time of night."

' "The creature passed by us just as we came out of the wood," said the female, in a silvery tone.

' "I was nearly discharging my piece at it," observed the hunter; "but since it did us such good service, I'm glad that I allowed it to escape."

'In about an hour and a half, during which my father walked at a rapid pace, the party arrived at the cottage, and, as I said before, came in.

' "We are in good time, apparently," observed the dark hunter, catching the smell of the roasted meat, as he walked to the fire and surveyed my brother and sister and myself. "You have young cooks here, Meinheer." "I am glad that we shall not have to wait," replied my father. "Come, mistress, seat yourself by the fire; you require warmth after your cold ride." "And where can I put up my horse, Meinheer?" observed the huntsman. "I will take care of him," replied my father, going out of the cottage door.

'The female, must, however, be particularly described. She was young, and apparently twenty years of age. She was dressed in a travelling dress, deeply bordered with white fur, and wore a cap of white ermine on her head. Her features were very beautiful, at least I thought so, and so my father has since declared. Her hair was flaxen, glossy, and shining, and bright as a mirror; and her mouth, although somewhat large when it was open, showed the most brilliant teeth I have ever beheld. But there was something about her eyes, bright as they were, which made us children afraid; they were so restless, so furtive; I could not at that time tell why, but I felt as if there was cruelty in her eye; and when she beckoned us to come to her, we approached her with fear and trembling. Still she was beautiful, very beautiful. She spoke kindly to my brother and myself, patted our heads and caressed us; but Marcella would not come near her; on the contrary, she slunk away, and hid herself in the bed, and would not wait for the supper, which half an hour before she had been so anxious for.

'My father, having put the horse into a close shed, soon returned, and supper was placed on the table. When it was over, my father requested the young lady would take possession of the bed, and he would remain at the fire, and sit up with her father. After some hesitation on her part, this arrangement was agreed to, and I and my brother crept into the other bed with Marcella, for we had as yet always slept together.

'But we could not sleep; there was something so unusual, not only in seeing strange people, but in having those people sleep at the cottage, that we were bewildered. As for poor little Marcella, she was quiet, but I perceived that she trembled during the whole night, and sometimes I thought that she was checking a sob. My father had brought out some spirits, which he rarely used, and he and the strange hunter remained drinking and talking before the fire. Our ears were ready to catch the slightest whisper – so much was our curiosity excited.

' "You said you came from Transylvania?" observed my father.

' "Even so, Meinheer," replied the hunter. "I was a serf to the noble house of —; my master would insist upon my surrendering up my fair girl to his wishes; it ended in my giving him a few inches of my hunting-knife."

' "We are countrymen and brothers in misfortune," replied my father, taking the huntsman's hand and pressing it warmly.

' "Indeed! Are you then from that country?"

' "Yes; and I too have fled for my life. But mine is a melancholy tale."

' "Your name?" inquired the hunter.

' "Krantz."

' "What! Krantz of – –? I have heard your tale; you need not renew your grief by repeating it now. Welcome, most welcome, Meinheer, and, I may say, my worthy kinsman. I am your second cousin, Wilfred of Barnsdorf," cried the hunter, rising up and embracing my father.

'They filled their horn-mugs to the brim, and drank to one another after the German fashion. The conversation was then carried on in a low tone; all that we could collect from it was that our new relative and his daughter were to take up their abode in our cottage, at least for the present. In about an hour they both fell back in their chairs and appeared to sleep.

' "Marcella, dear, did you hear?" said my brother, in a low tone.

' "Yes," replied Marcella, in a whisper, "I heard all. Oh! brother, I cannot bear to look upon that woman – I feel so frightened."

'My brother made no reply, and shortly afterwards we were all three fast asleep.

'When we awoke the next morning, we found that the hunter's daughter had risen before us. I thought she looked more beautiful than ever. She came up to little Marcella and caressed her: the child burst into tears, and sobbed as if her heart would break.

'But not to detain you with too long a story, the huntsman and his daughter were accommodated in the cottage. My father and he went out hunting daily, leaving Christina with us. She performed all the household duties; was very kind to us children; and gradually the dislike even of little Marcella wore away. But a great change took place in my father; he appeared to have conquered his aversion to the sex, and was most attentive to Christina. Often, after her father and we were in bed, he would sit up with her, conversing in a low tone by the fire. I ought to have mentioned that my father and the huntsman Wilfred slept in another portion of the cottage, and that the bed which he formerly occupied, and which was in the same room as ours, had been given up to the use of Christina. These visitors had been about three weeks at the cottage, when, one night, after we children had been sent to bed, a consultation was held. My father had asked Christina in marriage, and had obtained both her consent and that of Wilfred; after this, a conversation took place, which was, as near as I can recollect, as follows: –

' "You may take my child, Meinheer Krantz, and my blessing with her, and I shall then leave you and seek some other habitation – it matters little where.'

' "Why not remain here, Wilfred?"

' "No, no, I am called elsewhere; let that suffice, and ask no more questions. You have my child."

' "I thank you for her, and will duly value her; but there is one difficulty."

' "I know what you would say; there is no priest here in this wild country; true; neither is there any law to

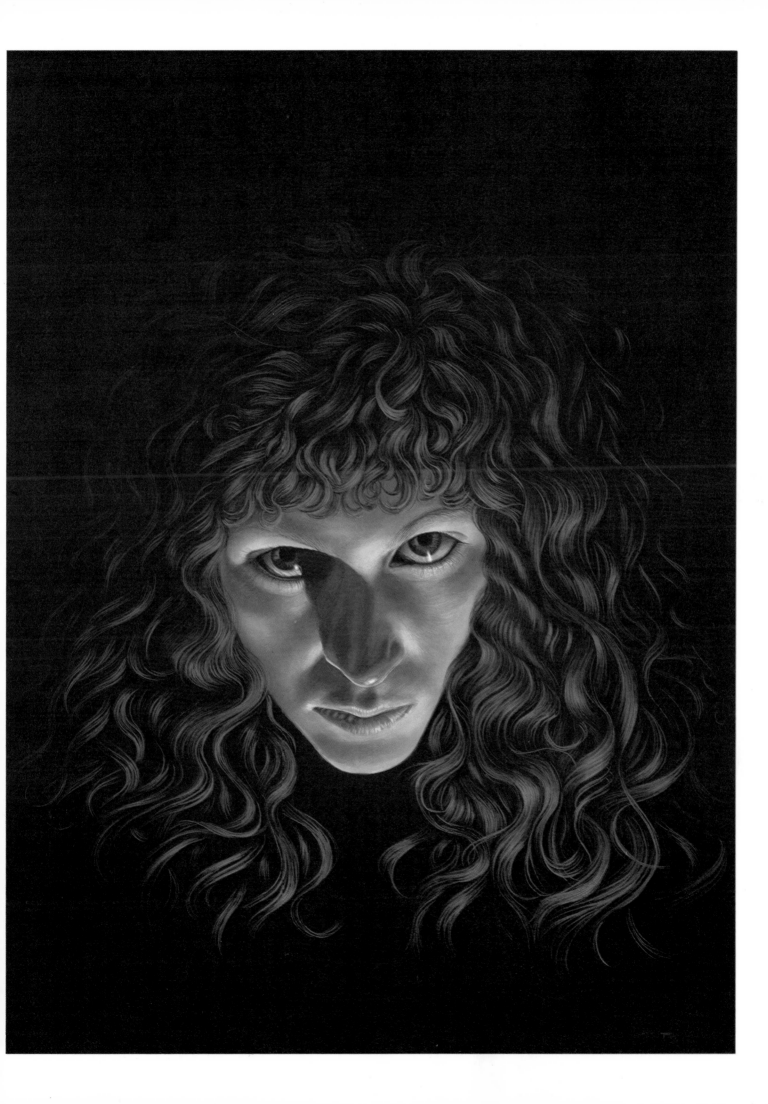

bind. Still must some ceremony pass between you to satisfy a father. Will you consent to marry her after my fashion? if so I will marry you directly."

' "I will," replied my father.

' "Then take her by the hand. Now, Meinheer, swear."

' "I swear," repeated my father.

' "By all the spirits of the Hartz Mountains —'

' "Nay, why not by Heaven?" interrupted my father.

' "Because it is not my humour," rejoined Wilfred. "If I prefer that oath, less binding, perhaps, than another, surely you will not thwart me."

' "Well, be it so, then; have your humour. Will you make me swear by that in which I do not believe?"

' "Yet many do so, who in outward appearance are Christians," rejoined Wilfred; "say, will you be married, or shall I take my daughter away with me?"

' "Proceed," replied my father impatiently.

' "I swear by all the spirits of the Hartz Mountains, by all the power for good or for evil, that I take Christina for my wedded wife; that I will ever protect her, cherish her, and love her; that my hand shall never be raised against her to harm her."

'My father repeated the words after Wilfred.

' "And if I fail in this my vow, may all the vengeance of the spirits fall upon me and upon my children; may they perish by the vulture, by the wolf, or other beasts of the forest; may their flesh be torn from their limbs, and their bones blanch in the wilderness: all this I swear."

' "My father hesitated, as he repeated the last words; little Marcella could not restrain herself, and as my father repeated the last sentence, she burst into tears. This sudden interruption appeared to discompose the party, particularly my father; he spoke harshly to the child, who controlled her sobs, burying her face under the bedclothes.

'Such was the second marriage of my father. The next morning, the hunter Wilfred mounted his horse and rode away.

'My father resumed his bed, which was in the same room as ours; and things went on much as before the marriage, except that our new mother-in-law did not show any kindness towards us; indeed, during my father's absence, she would often beat us, particularly little Marcella, and her eyes would flash fire, as she looked eagerly upon the fair and lovely child.

'One night my sister awoke me and my brother.

' "What is the matter?" said Cæsar.

' "She has gone out," whispered Marcella.

' "Gone out!"

' "Yes, gone out at the door, in her nightclothes," replied the child; "I saw her get out of bed, look at my father to see if he slept, and then she went out at the door."

'What could induce her to leave her bed, and all undressed, to go out, in such bitter wintry weather, with the snow deep on the ground, was to us incomprehensible; we lay awake, and in about an hour we heard the growl of a wolf close under the window.

' "There is a wolf," said Cæsar. "She will be torn to pieces."

' "Oh no!" cried Marcella.

'In a few minutes afterwards our mother-in-law appeared; she was in her night-dress, as Marcella had stated. She let down the latch of the door, so as to make no noise, went to a pail of water, and washed her face and hands, and then slipped into bed where my father lay.

' "We all three trembled – we hardly knew why; but we resolved to watch the next night. We did so; and not only on the ensuing night, but on many others, and always at about the same hour, would our mother-in-law rise from her bed and leave the cottage; and after she was gone we invariably heard the growl of a wolf under our window, and always saw her on her return wash herself before she retired to bed. We observed also that she seldom sat down to meals, and that when she did she appeared to eat with dislike; but when the meat was taken down to be prepared for dinner, she would often furtively put a raw piece into her mouth.

'My brother Cæsar was a courageous boy; he did not like to speak to my father until he knew more. He resolved that he would follow her out, and ascertain what she did. Marcella and I endeavoured to dissuade him from the project; but he would not be controlled; and the very next night he lay down in his clothes, and as soon as our mother-in-law had left the cottage he jumped up, took down my father's gun, and followed her.

'You may imagine in what a state of suspense Marcella and I remained during his absence. After a few minutes we heard the report of a gun. It did not awaken my father; and we lay trembling with anxiety. In a minute afterwards we saw our mother-in-law enter the cottage – her dress was bloody. I put my hand to Marcella's mouth to prevent her crying out, although I was myself in great alarm. Our mother-in-law approached my father's bed, looked to see if he was asleep, and then went to the chimney and blew up the embers into a blaze.

' "Who is there?" said my father, waking up.

' "Lie still, dearest," replied my mother-in-law; "it is only me; I have lighted the fire to warm some water; I am not quite well."

'My father turned round, and was soon asleep; but we watched our mother-in-law. She changed her linen, and threw the garments she had worn into the fire; and we then perceived that her right leg was bleeding profusely, as if from a gun-shot wound. She bandaged it up, and then dressing herself, remained before the fire until the break of day.

'Poor little Marcella, her heart beat quick as she pressed me to her side – so indeed did mine. Where was our brother Cæsar? How did my mother-in-law receive the wound unless from his gun? At last my father rose, and then for the first time I spoke saying,, "Father, where is my brother Cæsar?"

' "Your brother?" exclaimed he; "why, where can be be?"

' "Merciful Heaven! I thought as I lay very restless last night," observed our mother-in-law, "that I heard somebody open the latch of the door; and, dear me, husband, what has become of your gun?"

'My father cast his eyes up above the chimney, and perceived that his gun was missing. For a moment he looked perplexed; then, seizing a broad axe, he went out of the cottage without saying another word.

'He did not remain away from us long; in a few minutes he returned, bearing in his arms the mangled body of my poor brother; he laid it down and covered up his face.

'My mother-in-law rose up, and looked at the body, while Marcella and I threw ourselves by its side, wailing and sobbing bitterly.

' "Go to bed again, children," said she sharply. "Husband," continued she, "your boy must have taken the gun down to shoot a wolf, and the animal has been too powerful for him. Poor boy! he has paid dearly for his rashness."

'My father made no reply. I wished to speak – to tell all – but Marcella, who perceived my intention, held me by the arm, and looked at me so imploringly, that I desisted.

'My father, therefore, was left in his error; but Marcella and I, although we could not comprehend it, were conscious that our mother-in-law was in some way connected with my brother's death.

'That day my father went out and dug a grave; and when he laid the body in the earth, he piled stones over it, so that the wolves should not be able to dig it up. The shock of this catastrophe was to my poor father very severe; for several days he never went to the chase, although at times he would utter bitter anathemas and vengeance against the wolves.

'But during this time of mourning on his part, my mother-in-law's nocturnal wanderings continued with the same regularity as before.

'At last my father took down his gun to repair to the forest; but he soon returned, and appeared much annoyed.

' "Would you believe it, Christina, that the wolves – perdition to the whole race! – have actually contrived to dig up the body of my poor boy, and now there is nothing left of him but his bones."

' "Indeed!" replied my mother-in-law. Marcella looked at me, and I saw in her intelligent eye all she would have uttered.

' "A wolf growls under our window every night, father," said I.

' "Ay, indeed! Why did you not tell me, boy? Wake me the next time you hear it."

'I saw my mother-in-law turn away; her eyes flashed fire, and she gnashed her teeth.

'My father went out again, and covered up with a larger pile of stones the little remains of my poor brother which the wolves had spared. Such was the first act of the tragedy.

'The spring now came on; the snow disappeared, and we were permitted to leave the cottage; but never would I quit for one moment my dear little sister, to whom, since the death of my brother, I was more ardently attached than ever; indeed, I was afraid to leave her alone with my mother-in-law, who appeared to have a particular pleasure in ill-treating the child. My father was now employed upon his little farm, and I was able to render him some assistance.

'Marcella used to sit by us while we were at work, leaving my mother-in-law alone in the cottage. I ought to observe that, as the spring advanced, so did my mother-in-law decrease her nocturnal rambles, and that we never heard the growl of the wolf under the window after I had spoken of it to my father.

'One day, when my father and I were in the field, Marcella being with us, my mother-in-law came out, saying that she was going into the forest to collect some herbs my father wanted, and that Marcella must go to the cottage and watch the dinner. Marcella went; and my mother-in-law soon disappeared in the forest, taking a direction quite contrary to that in which the cottage stood, and leaving my father and me, as it were, between her and Marcella.

'About an hour afterwards we were startled by shrieks from the cottage – evidently the shrieks of little Marcella. "Marcella has burnt herself, father," said I, throwing down my spade. My father threw down his, and we both hastened to the cottage. Before we could gain the door, out darted a large white wolf, which fled with the utmost celerity. My father had no weapon; he rushed into the cottage, and there saw poor little Marcella expiring. Her body was dreadfully mangled and the blood pouring from it had formed a large pool on the cottage floor. My father's first intention had been to seize his gun and pursue; but he was checked by this horrid spectacle; he knelt down by his dying child, and burst into tears. Marcella could just look kindly on us for a few seconds, and then her eyes were closed in death.

'My father and I were still hanging over my poor sister's body, when my mother-in-law came in. At the dreadful sight she expressed much concern; but she did not appear to recoil from the sight of blood, as most women do.

' "Poor child!" said she, "it must have been that great white wolf which passed me just now, and frightened me so. She's quite dead, Krantz."

' "I know it! – I know it!" cried my father, in agony.

'I thought my father would never recover from the effects of this second tragedy; he mourned bitterly over the body of his sweet child, and for several days would not consign it to its grave, although frequently requested by my mother-in-law to do so. At last he yielded, and dug a grave for her close by that of my poor brother, and took every precaution that the wolves should not violate her remains.

'I was now really miserable as I lay alone in the bed which I had formerly shared with my brother and sister. I could not help thinking that my mother-in-law was implicated in both their deaths, although I could not account for the manner; but I no longer felt afraid of her; my little heart was full of hatred and revenge.

'The night after my sister had been buried, as I lay awake, I perceived my mother-in-law get up and go out of the cottage. I waited some time, then dressed myself, and looked out through the door, which I half opened. The moon shone bright, and I could see the spot where my brother and sister had been buried; and what was my horror when I perceived my mother-in-law busily removing the stones from Marcella's grave!

'She was in her white night-dress, and the moon shone full upon her. She was digging with her hands, and throwing away the stones behind her with all the ferocity of a wild beast. It was some time before I could collect my senses and decide what I should do. At last I perceived that she had arrived at the body, and raised it up to the side of the grave. I could bear it no longer: I ran to my father and awoke him.

' "Father, father!" cried I, "dress yourself, and get your gun."

' "What!" cried my father, "the wolves are there, are they?"

'He jumped out of bed, threw on his clothes, and in his anxiety did not appear to perceive the absence of his wife. As soon as he was ready I opened the door, he went out, and I followed him.

'Imagine his horror, when (unprepared as he was for such a sight) he beheld, as he advanced towards the grave, not a wolf, but his wife, in her night-dress, on her hands and knees, crouching by the body of my sister, and tearing off large pieces of the flesh, and devouring them with all the avidity of a wolf. She was too busy to be aware of our approach. My father dropped his gun; his hair stood on end, so did mine; he breathed heavily, and then his breath for a time stopped. I picked up the gun and put it into his hand. Suddenly he appeared as if concentrated rage had restored him to double vigour; he levelled his piece, fired, and with a loud shriek down fell the wretch whom he had fostered in his bosom.

' "God of heaven!" cried my father, sinking down upon the earth in a swoon, as soon as he had discharged his gun.

'I remained some time by his side before he recovered. "Where am I?" said he, "what has happened? Oh! – yes, yes! I recollect now. Heaven forgive me!"

'He rose and we walked up to the grave; what again was our astonishment and horror to find that, instead of the dead body of my mother-in-law, as we expected, there was lying over the remains of my poor sister a large white she-wolf.

' "The white wolf," exclaimed my father, "the white wolf which decoyed me into the forest – I see it all now – I have dealt with the spirits of the Hartz Mountains."

'For some time my father remained in silence and deep thought. He then carefully lifted up the body of my sister, replaced it in the grave, and covered it over as before, having struck the head of the dead animal with the heel of his boot, and raving like a madman. He walked back to the cottage, shut the door, and threw himself on the bed; I did the same, for I was in a stupor of amazement.

'Early in the morning we were both roused by a loud knocking at the door, and in rushed the hunter Wilfred.

' "My daughter – man – my daughter! – where is my daughter?" cried he in a rage.

' "Where the wretch, the fiend should be, I trust," replied my father, starting up, and displaying equal choler: "where she should be – in hell! Leave this cottage, or you may fare worse."

' "Ha – ha!" replied the hunter, "would you harm a potent spirit of the Hartz Mountains? Poor mortal, who must needs wed a werewolf."

' "Out, demon! I defy thee and thy power."

' "Yet shall you feel it; remember your oath – your solemn oath – never to raise your hand against her to harm her."

' "I made no compact with evil spirits."

' "You did, and if you failed in your vow, you were to meet the vengeance of the spirits. Your children were to perish by the vulture, the wolf –"

' "Out, out, demon!"

' "And their bones blanch in the wilderness. Ha! – ha!"

'My father, frantic with rage, seized his axe and raised it over Wilfred's head to strike.

' "All this I swear," continued the huntsman mockingly.

'The axe descended; but it passed through the form of the hunter, and my father lost his balance, and fell heavily on the floor.

'"Mortal!" said the hunter, striding over my father's body, "we have power over those only who have committed murder. You have been guilty of a double murder: you shall pay the penalty attached to your marriage vow. Two of your children are gone, the third is yet to follow – and follow them he will, for your oath is registered. Go – it were kindness to kill thee – your punishment is, that you live!"

'With these words the spirit disappeared. My father rose from the floor, embraced me tenderly, and knelt down in prayer.

'The next morning he quitted the cottage for ever. He took me with him, and bent his steps to Holland, where we safely arrived. He had some little money with him; but he had not been many days in Amsterdam before he was seized with a brain fever, and died raving mad. I was put into the asylum, and afterwards was sent to sea before the mast. The question is, whether I am to pay the penalty of my father's oath? I am myself perfectly convinced that, in some way or another, I shall.'

61

The Midnight Embrace
Matthew Lewis

Lewis was born into a wealthy family with estates in Jamaica, in 1775.
As a young man, he travelled in Germany and was influenced by Goethe.
He acquired fame upon publication of his novel, 'The Monk', mixed in
fashionable circles, and, for a time, was a Member of Parliament.
Although not an emancipationist, he was concerned for the welfare of the
slaves on his Jamaican estates. While returning from a visit to Jamaica,
in 1818, he died of yellow fever and was buried at sea.

Albert, lord of the ancient castle of Werdendorff, on the borders of the Black Forest, was a nobleman of elegant person, and fascinating manners; but his heart was prone to deceit. He was well versed in all the wily arts of seduction, and he paid slight attention to the fulfilling of either religious or moral duties, when opposed as a bar to his pleasures.

At the distance of half a league from his stately abode, resided the fair Josephine in an humble cottage, happy, virtuous, and respected. Beauty and innocence were the only dower she possessed. Her father had been a subaltern officer in the emperor's service. Her mother was the only child of a very poor, but very respectable pastor. Francisco, her father, had fallen in the field of battle when she had attained her fifth year. His disconsolate widow retired with her trifling pension from Vienna, where she had hitherto resided, to the vicinity of Werdendorff, where she lived with her darling child in a peaceful and retired seclusion now so congenial to their feelings. The education of Josephine she attended to with the most sedulous care, and was amply repaid by the docility of her pupil. At the age of sixteen, Josephine lost her parent, who, previous to her dissolution, gave every advice that a virtuous mind could dictate, with regard to the subsequent conduct of her daughter. Josephine listened to her virtuous counsels with attention, and while the pearly drops chased each other down her pallid cheeks, promised a strict adherence to the wishes of the dying parent. Alas! how little to be depended upon are the promises and resolutions of mortals!

The remains of the mother of Josephine being decently interred, the sorrowing girl soon felt herself obliged to grant less indulgence to heartfelt grief, that she might toil for each day's bread. Her parent's pension expired with her; and our fair maid, to pay the rent of her cottage, and defray her necessary expenditures, was obliged to leave her humble pallet with the first salute of the lark, and ply her needle with assiduous and unremitting industry. Her labour was crowned with success. She lived happy, virtuous, and respected, for the first three years after her mother's decease. She was then predestined to experience a fatal reverse: the veil of innocent simplicity was to be torn from her mind, and the vacancy filled up by the dark cloud of guilt.

Albert of Werdendorff beheld the maid in all her native pride of beauty, softened by angelic modesty, and her unconsciousness of the superlative charms she possessed. Albert longed to call this fair floweret his own; not as a tender admirer, to protect her honourably from all the storms of fate, but as a rude spoiler, that wantonly plucks the rose from its native branch, and then, regardless of its beauties, casts it to wither on the ground.

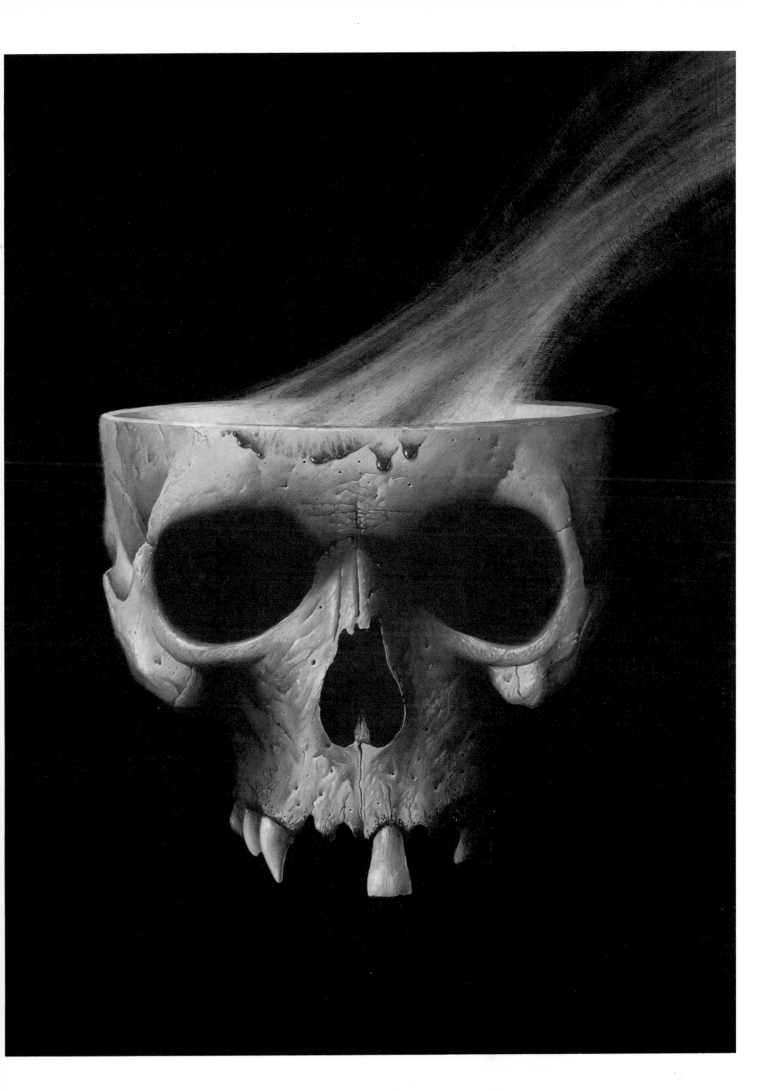

It is needless to describe minutely the various arts that Lord Albert descended to, in order to seduce the unsuspecting victim of his deceptions. His superior rank, fortune, and connections were so many circumstances to furnish him with favourable pretexts to forward his designs.

Though Albert was lord of the castle of Werdendorff, and had there a splendid establishment, yet he depended on his father for a princely addition to his possessions. He made Josephine to believe that it was impossible for him to espouse her during his father's life; but called on heaven, and every saint, to witness the inviolable faith and constancy he would always maintain towards her: that he should always regard her as his wife; and, as soon as he should be free to offer his hand, their marriage should be legally solemnized. Josephine had many virtuous sentiments; but Albert, by sophistry, overcame those scruples; and the unfortunate maiden added one more to the many that suffer their credulous hearts to be seduced by the wily serpent, like objects of their tender and faithful love.

Josephine's breast was no longer the abode of serenity. In Albert's presence her spirits were elated; she listened with delight to the repetition of his vows, and blinded by delusive passion, esteemed herself one of the happiest of the happy. But in the lone hours of solitude, she was oft times miserable. Regret, remorse, and apprehension, would enter, though obtrusive guests. From the casement of her cottage, Josephine could behold the stately castle of Werdendorff, and discern its portals opened for the reception of guests invited to the noble banquets and festive balls, which often made its lofty roofs resound with their mirth. On these occasions Josephine would sigh, and ponder on the wide difference between herself and Lord Albert in their stations, and wonder if her fond hopes would ever be realized.

At midnight, when all the inhabitants of the castle were wrapt in repose, was the time that Lord Albert paid his visits to Josephine's cottage, which hour was mutually chosen by the lovers for their interviews, that they might elude the observation of those around them. And when the moon gave no ray of light to Lord Albert

in his progress over the dark and fenny moor, Josephine would place a lighted taper at her casement, to guide him to her humble abode.

Ah! ill-fated maid! thou didst soon experience the dire truth, that men betray, and that vows can be broken; and that illicit love, though at first ardent, will soon decay, and leave nought but wretchedness behind.

Albert had been Josephine's favoured lover about six months, when, one hapless night, Josephine had placed the taper in her window as usual; and sat wishing the arrival of Albert in anxious expectation. More than once she conjectured she heard his well-known footsteps approach the door. She flew to open it, and her eye fixed on vacancy alone, while she shed bitter tears at the disappointment. Another, and another night elapsed; Albert came not; and Josephine's anguish and suspense became insupportable.

On the fourth morning of Albert's unusual absence, Josephine arose from her pallet after a few hours of restless and perturbed sleep; she approached the window, and her eyes taking their usual direction across the moor to the castle of Werdendorff, she beheld its gay banners streaming on the walls.

Anxious to learn the cause of this rejoicing, Josephine mingled with a group of rustic maidens who were repairing to the castle. She asked them, in tremulous accents, what propitious event they were celebrating at the Chateau; but the villagers were as ignorant as herself. When they came to the outer portal of the edifice, they beheld a gay procession passing from the hall to the chapel.

The sentinel, in reply to Josephine's interrogatories, informed her that Lord Albert was then gone to the chapel to seal his nuptial vows with Lady Guimilda, the proud daughter of a neighbouring baron, whose possessions were immense, and she the sole heiress.

Josephine replied not; her heart was full, even to bursting. She retreated from her companions, and seeking the covert of a friendly wood, gave way to all her frantic ravings of despair, which was still aggravated by every passing gale, bearing along the echoes of the loud shouts of revelry that pervaded the castle, and proclaimed Albert's perjury and her ruin.

As soon as the first violence of her grief was abated, she began to cherish delusive ideas. She thought the sentinel might have deceived her; or, at least, he might have been in an error himself, in supposing Lord Albert the bridegroom of the proud Guimilda; and she thought it more probable that it was some friend of his, who had solemnized his marriage at Werdendorff castle.

Cherishing this weak hope, she returned to her cottage; and partially disguising herself in a long mantle, and a thick white veil, she repaired at twilight to the castle, and, unobserved, mingled in the revelling crowd. But alas! the sentinel's intelligence she soon found to be too true; and the gayest among the gay throng was the false Albert and his bride Guimilda.

Once convinced, Josephine tarried no longer in the castle-hall. With torturing sensations, and faltering steps, she left the abode of her haughty rival, and once more sought her lonely dwelling. The night was dark, and the wind shook the rushes, and all around, like her own heart, was drear and forlorn. With folded arms, and her whole person like the statue of despair, sat Josephine by the casement. Fond recollections caused her tears to flow, when she called to mind how oft in that window she had placed the taper to light her then ardent lover over the moor.

While she was thus reflecting, she heard footsteps approach her cottage door; and presently she heard her own name softly pronounced. She instantly recognized Lord Albert's voice; and opening the casement, she cried indignantly, 'Away to Guimilda! Away to the pleasures that reign in Werdendorff castle. Why leave you my rival's bed, to add another insult to the woes you have caused me?'

Lord Albert renewed his entreaties for admission; and Josephine, at length, imprudently yielded to his request.

Albert exerted all his eloquence to convince the fair one, that his heart had no share in the nuptial contract with Guimilda; that there Josephine's image reigned triumphant, while her rival could claim nought but his hand. By the stern command of his father, he protested he had joined his fate to Guimilda's, who would only leave him his fortune on that condition: but that his love to Josephine should never be diminished by that circumstance; but that he would transplant her to a more pleasing abode, where she might reside in elegant retirement, and appear in a situation more congenial to his wishes than her present dwelling would allow, or, indeed, her near vicinity to the castle render prudent.

The soft blandishments of her deceiver again lured her to guile; and her anger was completely vanquished by love.

Again was the board spread with the choice delicacies, and delicious wines, that Lord Albert had brought with him from the castle; the flower-footed hours winged away with rapturous delight, and again the soft smile beamed on the lovely countenance of Josephine.

'Adieu, my beloved,' said Lord Albert; 'the first blush of morn empurples the east, and warns me from thy arms.'

Josephine inquired affectionately when she was next to expect her loved lord. He replied, that he would return at the *dark hour of midnight*, and again clasp her in his arms.

Lord Albert's bosom beat high as he sped homewards across the moor. The horrid deed he had committed, did not at that moment appal him. He congratulated himself on being freed from a mistress, whom satiety had for some time past made him detest.

In relating to Josephine the cause of his marriage with the Lady Guimilda, he had been guilty of a great falsehood. The known wealth of the heiress, at first, induced Lord Albert to visit at her father's villa; for avarice was a ruling passion with the youth. But when he beheld the haughty fair one, he instantly became a captive to her beauty, and loathed Josephine.

His nightly visits to Josephine, though conducted with much cautious secrecy, had by some means reached the ears of the proud Guimilda. No pity for the poor maiden filled her breast; she hated her fair rival, for having a prior claim to Lord Albert's heart. Her revengeful temper made her feel that she should never enjoy perfect happiness while Josephine existed. She thought that there was more than a probability, that, for all Albert's declarations to the contrary, when she conversed with him on the subject, that, after a short time would elapse, his heart might grow cold towards the legal partner of his fortune, and return with redoubled ardour to his deserted mistress. She knew the infirmities of her own temper; and the angelic sweetness of disposition which her informants had represented Josephine to possess, contrasted with her own hauteur, caprice, and tyranny, made the confirmation of her fears appear as strong as proofs of holy writ.

To glut her revenge, and leave no room for apprehension, she formed the horrid project of demanding the following sacrifice at the hands of Lord Albert.

This was the removal of Josephine by a poison which should take a quick effect, and cause her to breathe her last ere she should have time to reveal the name of her murderer. The time fixed on by Guimilda for the perpetration of this horrid deed, was their wedding night. Albert was to make some plausible excuse to his guests, to account for his absenting himself at that time, and then to repair to Josephine's cottage; and, as he always, on those occasions, condescended to convey with his own hands, some refreshments, it would be an easy matter for him to infuse into the goblet of wine that he should present to his fair victim, a deadly but tasteless drug that Guimilda prepared for that fatal purpose. The proud Guimilda made a solemn vow, never to admit Lord Albert to her bed, till her horrific demand was complied with.

Alas! her destined husband was too pliantly moulded to her purpose; he made not half the resistance she expected to encounter; but, after a very few scruples, signified his perfect acquiescence with the will of this fiend in female form.

How Lord Albert effected his purpose has been previously described. He had nearly gained the castle on his return, when his own words recurred to his memory: at the dark hour of midnight he would again return, and clasp her in his arms. 'Ill-fated Josephine!' exclaimed he, mentally. 'Ere that hour arrives, thy fluttering breath will flee amid agonizing pain; and thou, late so beauteous, wilt be a lifeless corpse.' The first light of morning cheerfully illumined the dell; but Albert's heart was not gladdened by the scene.

The beams of the sun began to gild the turrets of Werdendorff, yet the bridal ball was not concluded. In vain the blaze of beauty met Lord Albert's eyes; he sighed amid surrounding splendour; for conscience had strongly entwined her chains around his heart. Guimilda was impatient to know if her lord had accomplished the dire deed; and, on his answering in the affirmative, she experienced the most extravagant and unnatural transports. But Albert was clouded with horror; and he kept constantly repeating the words, 'At midnight's dark hour thou shalt embrace me again.'

On the next evening the guests again assembled in the halls of Werdendorff, again the musicians tuned their instruments to notes of joy; and again the gay knights and their fair partners joined in the mazy dance. Lord Albert alone seemed abstracted; and his woe-expressive countenance gave rise to a variety of conjectures, all very remote from the truth. Guimilda perceived the agony of his mind (which her hardened heart considered as a weakness) with extreme displeasure; nor was she slow in whispering to him the most keen reproaches for the pusillanimity of his conduct, in appearing in this manner before their guests.

But in vain Lord Albert endeavoured to arouse himself, and put on a gay unembarrassed air. His mind, in a few hours, had undergone a total revolution. He now regarded Guimilda as an agent of infernal malice, sent to plunge his soul into an irremediable abyss of guilt. The artless behaviour of his murdered love was the contrast; her gentle unupbraiding manners, the affectionate looks with which she would hang enraptured over him, and listen to the tender oaths he had so basely violated, was in these thoughts; yet they every moment rushed unbidden on his brain.

As midnight's dark hour was proclaimed by the turret bell, Albert's limbs shook with fear. 'I hear,' said he, aloud, 'the fatal summons that calls me hence. Guimilda, farewell for ever! this is thy work.'

Guimilda was going to make some reply, when a tremendous storm suddenly shook the battlements of the castle: the thunder's loud peals burst on the ancient walls, while the lightning's pointed glare flashed with appalling repetition through the painted casements. Dim burnt the numberless tapers, when Josephine's death-like form glided from the portal, and, with solemn pace, proceeded along the hall to the spot where Lord Albert stood. Pale was her face, and her features seemed to retain the convulsive marks of the horrid death to which Guimilda had revengefully consigned her. Clad in the habiliments of the grave, her appearance was awe-inspiring. In a hollow, deep-toned voice, she addressed her perjured lover:

'Thou false one! Base assassin of her whom thou lured'st from the flowery paths of virtue; her whom thou had'st sworn to cherish and protect while life was left thee. Thou hast cut short the thread of my existence: but think not to escape the punishment due to thy crimes. 'Tis midnight's dark hour; the hour by thyself appointed: delay not, therefore, thy promised embrace.'

With these words Josephine wound her arms around his trembling form. 'I am come from the confines of the dead,' said she, 'to make thee fulfil thy parting promise.' She dragged him by a force he could not resist to her breast: she pressed her clammy lips to his; and held him fast in her noisome icy embrace.

At length the horrific spectre released him from her grasp. He started back in breathless agony, and sank senseless on the floor. Thrice he raised his frenzied eye to gaze on his supernatural visitant; thrice he raised his hands, as if to implore the mercy of offended heaven; and then expired with a heavy groan.

Again loud thunder shook the castle to its very foundation. The affrighted guests rushed from the hall, rather choosing to brave the fury of the elements, than remain spectators of the horrid scene within its walls. Even the proud Guimilda fled with terror and dismay. She sought refuge in a convent that stood about a league's distance from the castle; here she remained till death put a period to her mental sufferings, which far exceeded her corporeal ones; though they were many, and severe; for she exhausted her frame by the variety and frequencies of the vigorous penance she imposed on herself, as a chastisement for her heinous, regretted crime.

As soon as Lord Albert's body was interred, the domestics hastily left the horrid castle. The edifice, being greatly damaged by the storm, soon fell to decay. Its dismantled ramparts were skirted with thorns; and the proud turrets of Werdendorff lay scattered on the plain.

Full oft, when the traveller wanders among the time-stricken ruins, a peasant will lead him to his cot, and relate the sad story of Albert and Josephine, and warn the stranger not to rove among the avenues of the castle, lest he should be assailed by the grim spectres, who always punish the temerity of those who intrude with un-hallowed steps in the mansion where they keep their mysterious orgies. The hall of the castle still remains entire amid the Gothic ruins. On the anniversary of that fatal night when Josephine's spectre gave the midnight embrace to the false Albert, the same scene is again acted by supernatural beings. Guimilda, her husband, and his murdered love, traverse the haunted hall, which is then illumined with a more than mortal light: and the groans of the spectre lord can be heard afar, while he is clasped in the arms of Josephine's implacable ghost.

Oft will the village maidens, at the sober gloom of evening, review the isolated scene, and relate to those of their juvenile companions, yet unacquainted with the tragic tale, all the particulars of that wondrous legend; while they shuddering pass the mouldering tomb that covers the libertine's remains, to weep over the lowly violet-covered grave of the fair, but frail Josephine.

The Devil's Wager
William Makepeace Thackeray

Thackeray was born in Calcutta in 1811. On the death of his father, an
official in the East India Company, he was sent to school in England.
He studied at Cambridge and the Middle Temple, but abandoned law for
the study of art. He lost a small fortune, partly through gambling, and, in
Paris, married a penniless Irish girl who eventually went insane. Like
Dickens, his close rival, he made frequent contributions to magazines.
He died in 1863.

It was the hour of the night when there be none stirring save churchyard ghosts – when all doors are closed except the gates of graves, and all eyes shut but the eyes of wicked men.

When there is no sound on the earth except the ticking of the grasshopper, or the croaking of obscene frogs in the pool.

And no light except that of the blinking stars, and the wicked and devilish wills-o'-the-wisp, as they gambol among the marshes, and lead good men astray.

When there is nothing moving in heaven except the owl, as he flappeth along lazily; or the magician, as he rideth on his infernal broomstick, whistling through the air like the arrows of a Yorkshire archer.

It was at this hour (namely, at twelve o'clock of the night,) that two things went winging through the black clouds, and holding converse with each other.

Now the first was Mercurius, the messenger, not of gods (as the heathens feigned), but of demons; and the second, with whom he held company, was the soul of Sir Roger de Rollo, the brave knight. Sir Roger was Count of Chauchigny, in Champagne; Seigneur of Santerre, Villacerf and autre lieux. But the great die as well as the humble; and nothing remained of brave Roger now, but his coffin and his deathless soul.

And Mercurius, in order to keep fast the soul, his companion, had bound him round the neck with his tail; which, when the soul was stubborn, he would draw so tight as to strangle him wellnigh, sticking into him the barbed point thereof; whereat the poor soul, Sir Rollo, would groan and roar lustily.

Now they two had come together from the gates of purgatory, being bound to those regions of fire and flame where poor sinners fry and roast *in saecula saeculorum*.

'It is hard,' said the poor Sir Rollo, as they went gliding through the clouds, 'that I should thus be condemned for ever, and all for want of a single ave.'

'How, Sir Soul?' said the demon. 'You were on earth so wicked, that not one, or a million of aves, could suffice to keep from hell-flame a creature like thee; but cheer up and be merry; thou wilt be but a subject of our lord the Devil, as am I; and, perhaps, thou wilt be advanced to posts of honour, as am I also:' and to show his authority, he lashed with his tail the ribs of the wretched Rollo.

'Nevertheless, sinner as I am, one more ave would have saved me; for my sister, who was Abbess of St. Mary of Chauchigny, did so prevail, by her prayer and good works, for my lost and wretched soul, that every day

I felt the pains of purgatory decrease; the pitchforks which, on my first entry, had never ceased to vex and torment my poor carcass, were now not applied above once a week; the roasting had ceased, the boiling had discontinued; only a certain warmth was kept up, to remind me of my situation.'

'A gentle stew,' said the demon.

'Yea, truly, I was but in a stew, and all from the effects of the prayers of my blessed sister. But yesterday, he who watched me in purgatory told me, that yet another prayer from my sister, and my bonds should be unloosed, and I, who am now a devil, should have been a blessed angel."

'And the other ave?' said the demon.

'She died, sir – my sister died – death choked her in the middle of the prayer.' And hereat the wretched spirit began to weep and whine piteously; his salt tears falling over his beard, and scalding the tail of Mercurius the devil.

'It is, in truth, a hard case,' said the demon; 'but I know of no remedy save patience, and for that you will have an excellent opportunity in your lodgings below.'

'But I have relations,' said the Earl; 'my kinsman Randal, who has inherited my lands, will he not say a prayer for his uncle?'

'Thou didst hate and oppress him when living.'

'It is true; but an ave is not much; his sister, my niece, Matilda –'

'You shut her in a convent, and hanged her lover.'

'Had I not reason? besides, has she not others?'

'A dozen, without a doubt.'

'And my brother, the prior?'

'A liege subject of my lord the Devil: he never opens his mouth, except to utter an oath, or to swallow a cup of wine.'

'And yet, if but one of these would but say an ave for me, I should be saved.'

'Aves with them are *rarae* aves,' replied Mercurius, wagging his tail right waggishly; 'and, what is more, I will lay thee any wager that no one of these will say a prayer to save thee.'

'I would wager willingly,' responded he of Chauchigny; 'but what has a poor soul like me to stake?'

'Every evening, after the day's roasting, my lord Satan giveth a cup of cold water to his servants; I will bet thee thy water for a year, that none of the three will pray for thee.'

'Done!' said Rollo.

'Done!' said the demon; and here, if I mistake not, is thy castle of Chauchigny.'

Indeed, it was true. The soul, on looking down, perceived the tall towers, the courts, the stables, and the fair gardens of the castle. Although it was past midnight, there was a blaze of light in the banqueting-hall, and a lamp burning in the open window of the Lady Matilda.

'With whom shall we begin?' said the demon: 'with the baron or the lady?'

'With the lady, if you will.'

'Be it so; her window is open, let us enter.'

So they descended, and entered silently into Matilda's chamber.

*   *   *

The young lady's eyes were fixed so intently on a little clock, that it was no wonder that she did not perceive the entrance of her two visitors. Her fair cheek rested in her white arm, and her white arm on the cushion of a great chair in which she sat, pleasantly supported by sweet thoughts and swan's down; a lute was at her side, and a book of prayers lay under the table (for piety is always modest). Like the amorous Alexander, she sighed and looked (at the clock) – and sighed for ten minutes or more, when she softly breathed the word 'Edward!'

At this the soul of the Baron was wroth. 'The jade is at her old pranks,' said he to the devil; and then addressing Matilda: 'I pray thee, sweet niece, turn thy thoughts for a moment from that villainous page, Edward, and give them to thine affectionate uncle.'

When she heard the voice, and saw the awful apparition of her uncle (for a year's sojourn in purgatory had not increased the comeliness of his appearance), she started, screamed, and of course fainted.

But the devil Mercurius soon restored her to herself. 'What's o'clock?' said she, as soon as she had recovered from her fit: 'is he come?'

'Not thy lover, Maude, but thine uncle – that is, his soul. For the love of heaven, listen to me: I have been frying in purgatory for a year past, and should have been in heaven but for the want of a single ave.'

'I will say it for thee tomorrow, uncle.'

'Tonight, or never.'

'Well, tonight be it:' and she requested the devil Mercurius to give her the prayer-book, from under the table; but he had no sooner touched the holy book than he dropped it with a shriek and a yell. 'It was hotter,' he said, 'than his master Sir Lucifer's own particular pitchfork.' And the lady was forced to begin her ave without the aid of her missal.

At the commencement of her devotions the demon retired, and carried with him the anxious soul of poor Sir Roger de Rollo.

The lady knelt down – she sighed deeply; she looked again at the clock, and began –

'Ave Maria.'

When a lute was heard under the window, and a sweet voice singing –

'Hark!' said Matilda.

> 'Now the toils of day are over,
>   And the sun hath sunk to rest,
> Seeking, like a fiery lover,
>   The bosom of the blushing west –
>
> 'The faithful night keeps watch and ward,
>   Raising the moon, her silver shield,
> And summoning the stars to guard
>   The slumbers of my fair Mathilde!'

'For mercy's sake!' said Sir Rollo, 'the ave first, and next the song.'

So Matilda again dutifully betook her to her devotions, and began –

'Ave Maria gratia plena!' but the music began again, and the prayer ceased of course.

> 'The faithful night! Now all things lie
>   Hid by her mantle dark and dim,
> In pious hope I hither hie,
>   And humbly chant mine ev'ning hymn.
>
> 'Thou art my prayer, my saint, my shrine!
>   (For never holy pilgrim kneel'd,
> Or wept at feet more pure than mine),
>   My virgin love, my sweet Mathilde!'

'Virgin love!' said the Baron. 'Upon my soul, this is too bad!' and he thought of the lady's lover whom he had caused to be hanged.

But *she* only thought of him who stood singing at her window.

'Niece Matilda!' cried Sir Roger, agonizedly, 'wilt thou listen to the lies of an impudent page, whilst thine uncle is waiting but a dozen words to make him happy?'

At this Matilda grew angry: 'Edward is neither impudent nor a liar, Sir Uncle, and I will listen to the end of the song.'

'Come away,' said Mercurius; 'he hath yet got wield, field, sealed, congealed, and a dozen other rhymes beside; and after the song will come the supper.'

So the poor soul was obliged to go; while the lady listened, and the page sung away till morning.

*　　　*　　　*

'My virtues have been my ruin,' said poor Sir Rollo, as he and Mercurius slunk silently out of the window. 'Had I hanged that knave Edward, as I did the page his predecessor, my niece would have sung mine ave, and I should have been by this time an angel in heaven.'

'He is reserved for wiser purposes,' responded the devil: 'he will assassinate your successor, the lady Mathilde's brother; and, in consequence, will be hanged. In the love of the lady he will be succeeded by a gardener, who will be replaced by a monk, who will give way to an ostler, who will be deposed by a Jew pedlar, who shall, finally, yield to a noble earl, the future husband of the fair Mathilde. So that, you see, instead of having one poor soul a-frying, we may now look forward to a goodly harvest for our lord the Devil.'

The soul of the Baron began to think that his companion knew too much for one who would make fair bets; but there was no help for it; he would not, and he could not cry off: and he prayed inwardly that the brother might be found more pious than the sister.

But there seemed little chance of this. As they crossed the court, lackeys, with smoking dishes and full jugs, passed and repassed continually, although it was long past midnight. On entering the hall, they found Sir Randal at the head of a vast table, surrounded by a fiercer and more motley collection of individuals than had congregated there even in the time of Sir Rollo. The lord of the castle had signified that 'it was his royal pleasure to be drunk,' and the gentlemen of his train had obsequiously followed their master. Mercurius was delighted with the scene, and relaxed his usually rigid countenance into a bland and benevolent smile, which became him wonderfully.

The entrance of Sir Roger, who had been dead about a year, and a person with hoofs, horns, and a tail, rather disturbed the hilarity of the company. Sir Randal dropped his cup of wine; and Father Peter, the confessor, incontinently paused in the midst of a profane song, with which he was amusing the society.

'Holy Mother!' cried he, 'it is Sir Roger.'

'Alive!' screamed Sir Randal.

'No, my lord,' Mercurius said; 'Sir Roger is dead, but cometh on a matter of business; and I have the honour to act as his counsellor and attendant.'

'Nephew,' said Sir Roger, 'the demon saith justly; I am come on a trifling affair, in which thy service is essential.'

'I will do anything, uncle, in my power.'

'Thou canst give me life, if thou wilt?' But Sir Randal looked very blank at this proposition. 'I mean life spiritual, Randal,' said Sir Roger; and thereupon he explained to him the nature of the wager.

Whilst he was telling his story, his companion Mercurius was playing all sorts of antics in the hall; and, by his wit and fun, became so popular with this godless crew, that they lost all the fear which his first appearance had given them. The friar was wonderfully taken with him, and used his utmost eloquence and endeavours to convert the devil; the knights stopped drinking to listen to the argument; the men-at-arms forbore brawling; and the wicked little pages crowded round the two strange disputants, to hear their edifying discourse. The ghostly man, however, had little chance in the controversy, and certainly little learning to carry it on. Sir Randal interrupted him. 'Father Peter,' said he, 'our kinsman is condemned for ever, for want of a single ave: wilt thou say it for him?' 'Willingly, my lord,' said the monk, 'with my book;' and accordingly he produced his missal to read, without which aid it appeared that the holy father could not manage the desired prayer. But the crafty Mercurius had, by his devilish art, inserted a song in the place of the ave, so that Father Peter, instead of chanting a hymn, sang the following irreverent ditty:

'Some love the matin-chimes, which tell
    The hour of prayer to sinner:
But better far's the mid-day bell,
    Which speaks the hour of dinner;
For when I see a smoking fish,
    Or capon drowned in gravy,
Or noble haunch on silver dish,
    Full glad I sing mine ave.

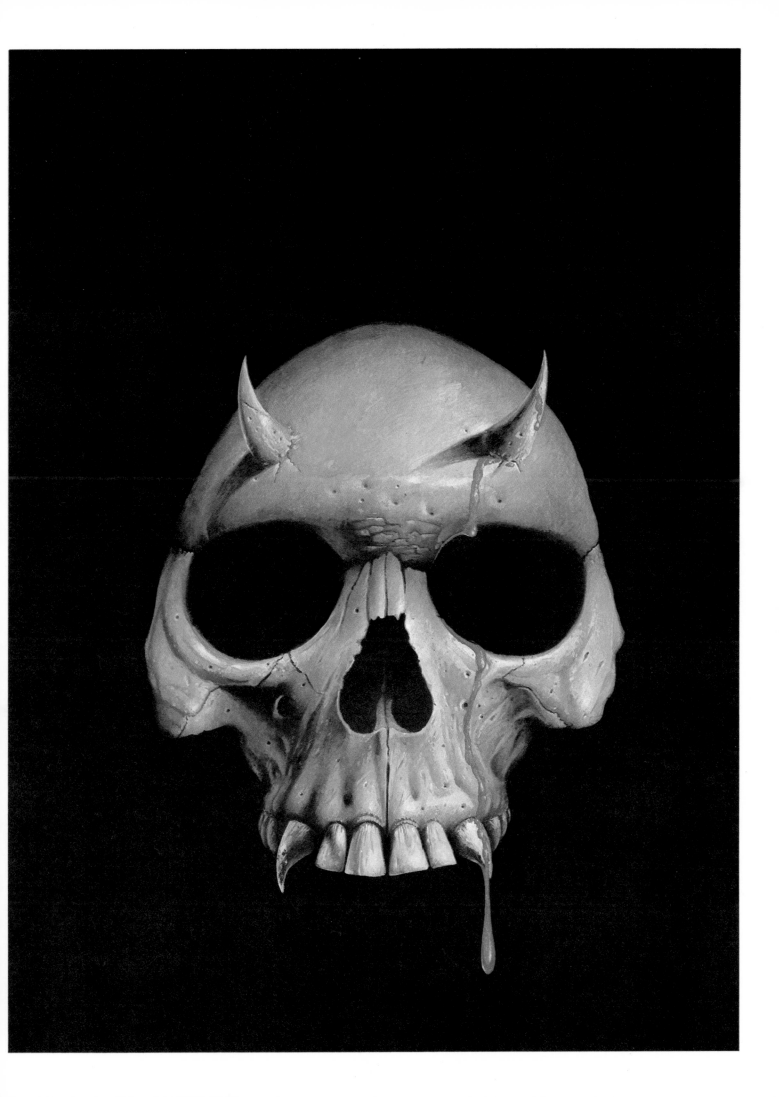

'My pulpit is an ale-house bench,
  Whereon I sit so jolly;
A smiling rosy country wench
  My saint and patron holy.
I kiss her cheek so red and sleek,
  I press her ringlets wavy.
And in her willing ear I speak
  A most religious ave.

'And if I'm blind, yet heaven is kind,
  And holy saints forgiving;
For sure he leads a right good life
  Who thus admires good living.
Above they say, our flesh is air,
  Our blood celestial ichor:
Oh, grant! mid all the changes there,
  They may not change our liquor!'

And with this pious wish the holy confessor tumbled under the table in an agony of devout drunkenness; whilst the knights, the men-at-arms, and the wicked little pages, rang out the last verse with a most melodious and emphatic glee. 'I am sorry, fair uncle,' hiccupped Sir Randal, 'that, in the matter of the ave, we could not oblige thee in a more orthodox manner; but the holy father has failed, and there is not another man in the hall who hath an idea of a prayer.'

'It is my own fault,' said Sir Rollo; 'for I hanged the last confessor.' And he wished his nephew a surly goodnight, as he prepared to quit the room.

'Au revoir, gentlemen,' said the devil Mercurius; and once more fixed his tail round the neck of his disappointed companion.

The spirit of poor Rollo was sadly cast down; the devil, on the contrary, was in high good humour. He wagged his tail with the most satisfied air in the world, and cut a hundred jokes at the expense of his poor associate. On they sped, cleaving swiftly through the cold night winds, frightening the birds that were roosting in the woods, and the owls that were watching in the towers.

In the twinkling of an eye, as it is known, devils can fly hundreds of miles: so that almost the same beat of the clock which left these two in Champagne found them hovering over Paris. They dropped into the court of the Lazarist Convent, and winded their way, through passage and cloister, until they reached the door of the prior's cell.

Now the prior, Rollo's brother, was a wicked and malignant sorcerer; his time was spent in conjuring devils and doing wicked deeds, instead of fasting, scourging, and singing holy psalms: this Mercurius knew; and he, therefore, was fully at ease as to the final result of his wager with poor Sir Roger.

'You seem to be well acquainted with the road,' said the knight.

'I have reason,' answered Mercurius, 'having, for a long period, had the acquaintance of his reverence, your brother; but you have little chance with him.'

'And why?' said Sir Rollo.

'He is under a bond to my master, never to say a prayer, or else his soul and his body are forfeited at once.'

'Why, thou false and traitorous devil!' said the enraged knight; 'and thou knewest this when we made our wager?'

'Undoubtedly: do you suppose I would have done so had there been any chance of losing?'

And with this they arrived at Father Ignatius's door.

'Thy cursed presence threw a spell on my niece, and stopped the tongue of my nephew's chaplain; I do believe that had I seen either of them alone, my wager had been won.'

'Certainly; therefore, I took good care to go with thee; however, thou mayest see the prior alone, if thou wilt; and lo! his door is open. I will stand without for five minutes when it will be time to commence our journey.'

It was the poor Baron's last chance: and he entered his brother's room more for the five minutes' respite than from any hope of success.

Father Ignatius, the prior, was absorbed in magic calculations: he stood in the middle of a circle of skulls, with no garment except his long white beard, which reached to his knees; he was waving a silver rod, and muttering imprecations in some horrible tongue.

But Sir Rollo came forward and interrupted his incantation. 'I am,' said he, 'the shade of thy brother Roger de Rollo; and have come, from pure brotherly love, to warn thee of thy fate.'

'Whence camest thou?'

'From the abode of the blessed in Paradise,' replied Sir Roger, who was inspired with a sudden thought; 'it was but five minutes ago that the Patron Saint of thy church told me of thy danger, and of thy wicked compact with the fiend. "Go," said he, "to thy miserable brother, and tell him there is but one way by which he may escape from paying the awful forfeit of his bond." '

'And how may that be?' said the prior; 'the false fiend hath deceived me; I have given him my soul, but have received no worldly benefit in return. Brother! dear brother! how may I escape?'

'I will tell thee. As soon as I heard the voice of blessed St. Mary Lazarus' (the worthy Earl had, at a pinch, coined the name of a saint), 'I left the clouds, where, with other angels, I was seated, and sped hither to save thee. "Thy brother," said the Saint, "hath but one day more to live, when he will become for all eternity the subject of Satan; if he would escape, he must boldly break his bond, by saying an ave." '

'It is the express condition of the agreement,' said the unhappy monk, 'I must say no prayer, or that instant I become Satan's, body and soul.'

'It is the express condition of the Saint,' answered Roger, fiercely; 'pray, brother, pray, or thou art lost for ever.'

So the foolish monk knelt down, and devoutly sung out an ave. 'Amen!' said Sir Roger, devoutly.

'Amen!' said Mercurius, as, suddenly, coming behind, he seized Ignatius by his long beard, and flew up with him to the top of the church-steeple.

The monk roared, and screamed, and swore against his brother; but it was of no avail: Sir Roger smiled kindly on him, and said, 'Do not fret, brother; it must have come to this in a year or two.'

And he flew alongside of Mercurius to the steeple-top; *but this time the devil had not his tail round his neck*. 'I will let thee off thy bet,' said he to the demon; for he could afford, now, to be generous.

'I believe, my lord,' said the demon, politely, 'that our ways separate here.' Sir Roger sailed gaily upwards: while Mercurius having bound the miserable monk faster than ever, he sunk downwards to earth, and perhaps lower. Ignatius was heard roaring and screaming as the devil dashed him against the iron spikes and buttresses of the church.

The Monkey's Paw
W.W.Jacobs

W. W. Jacobs was born in 1863 in Wapping. His father worked on the wharves and his experiences as a child provided him with a wealth of material for the stories he would later write. As a young man he became a Civil Servant, and his recollection of childhood poverty made him reticent to leave this employ until his economic future as a writer was secure. He is mainly remembered for his short stories about sailors, country life, and the macabre. He died in 1943.

Without, the night was cold and wet, but in the small parlour of Laburnum Villa the blinds were drawn and the fire burned brightly. Father and son were at chess; the former, who possessed ideas about the game involving radical changes, putting his king into such sharp and unnecessary perils, that it even provoked comment from the white-haired old lady knitting placidly by the fire.

'Hark at the wind,' said Mr. White, who, having seen a fatal mistake after it was too late, was amiably desirous of preventing his son from seeing it.

'I'm listening,' said the latter, grimly surveying the board as he stretched out his hand. 'Check.'

'I should hardly think that he'd come tonight,' said his father, with his hand poised over the board.

'Mate,' replied the son.

'That's the worst of living so far out,' bawled Mr. White, with sudden and unlooked-for violence; 'of all the beastly, slushy, out-of-the-way places to live in, this is the worst. Path's a bog, and road's a torrent. I don't know what people are thinking about. I suppose because only two houses in the road are let, they think it doesn't matter.'

'Never mind, dear,' said his wife, soothingly; 'perhaps you will win the next one.'

Mr. White looked up sharply, just in time to intercept a knowing glance between mother and son. The words died away on his lips, and he hid a guilty grin in his thin grey beard.

'There he is,' said Herbert White, as the gate banged to loudly and heavy footsteps came towards the door.

The old man rose with hospitable haste, and opening the door, was heard condoling with the new arrival. The new arrival also condoled with himself, so that Mrs. White said, 'Tut, Tut!' and coughed gently as her husband entered the room, followed by a tall, burly man, beady of eye and rubicund of visage.

'Sergeant-Major Morris,' he said, introducing him.

The sergeant-major shook hands, and taking the proffered seat by the fire, watched contentedly while his host got out whisky and tumblers and stood a small copper kettle on the fire.

At the third glass his eyes got brighter, and he began to talk, the little family circle regarding with eager interest this visitor from distant parts, as he squared his broad shoulders in the chair and spoke of wild scenes and doughty deeds; of wars and plagues and strange peoples.

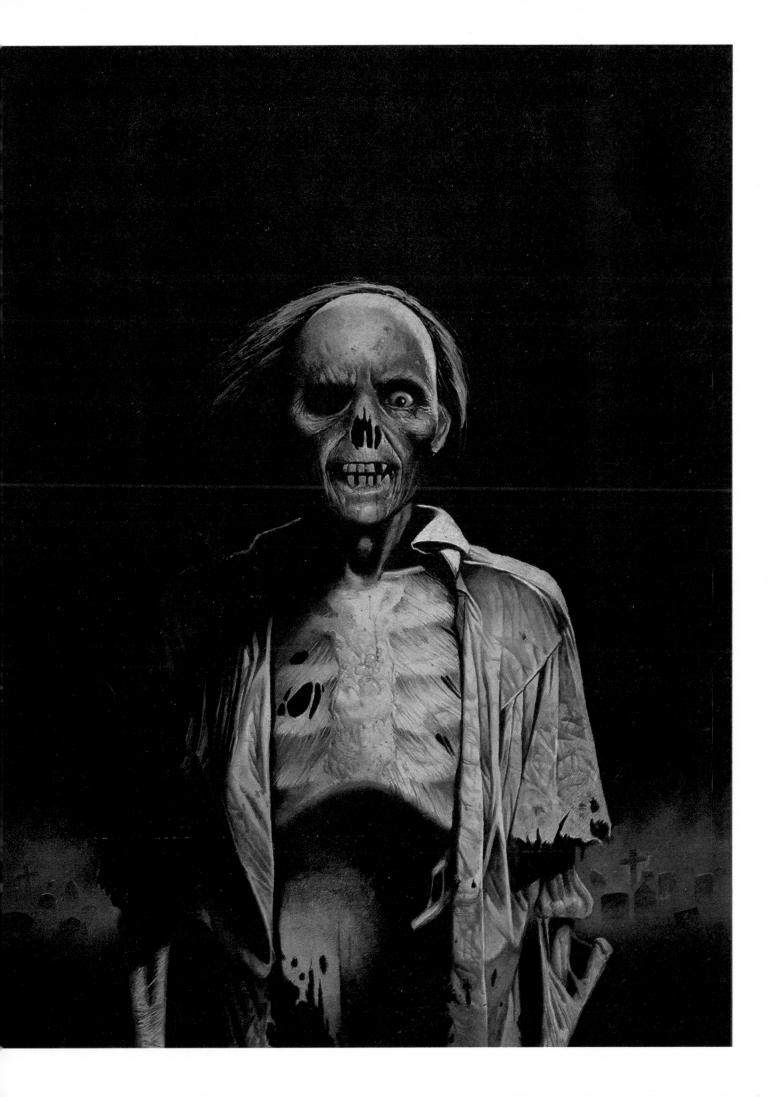

'Twenty-one years of it,' said Mr. White, nodding at his wife and son. 'When he went away he was a slip of a youth in the warehouse. Now look at him.'

'He don't look to have taken much harm,' said Mrs. White politely.

'I'd like to go to India myself,' said the old man, 'just to look around a bit, you know.'

'Better where you are,' said the sergeant-major, shaking his head. He put down the empty glass, and, sighing softly, shook his head again.

'I should like to see those old temples and fakirs and jugglers,' said the old man. 'What was that you started telling me the other day about a monkey's paw or something, Morris?'

'Nothing,' said the soldier hastily. 'Leastways nothing worth hearing.'

'Monkey's paw?' said Mrs. White curiously.

'Well, it's just a bit of what you might call magic, perhaps,' said the sergeant-major, offhandedly.

His three listeners leaned forward eagerly. The visitor absentmindedly put his empty glass to his lips and then set it down again. His host filled it for him.

'To look at,' said the sergeant-major, fumbling in his pocket, 'it's just an ordinary little paw, dried to a mummy.'

He took something out of his pocket and proffered it. Mrs. White drew back with a grimace, but her son, taking it, examined it curiously.

'And what is there special about it?' inquired Mr. White as he took it from his son, and having examined it, placed it upon the table.

'It had a spell put on it by an old fakir,' said the sergeant-major, 'a very holy man. He wanted to show that fate ruled people's lives, and that those who interfered with it did so to their sorrow. He put a spell on it so that three separate men could each have three wishes from it.'

His manner was so impressive that his hearers were conscious that their light laughter jarred somewhat.

'Well, why don't you have three, sir?' said Herbert White, cleverly.

The soldier regarded him in the way that middle age is wont to regard presumptuous youth. 'I have,' he said quietly, and his blotchy face whitened.

'And did you really have the three wishes granted?' asked Mrs. White.

'I did,' said the sergeant-major, and his glass tapped against his strong teeth.

'And has anybody else wished?' persisted the old lady.

'The first man had his three wishes. Yes,' was the reply. 'I don't know what the first two were, but the third was for death. That's how I got the paw.'

His tones were so grave that a hush fell upon the group.

'If you've had your three wishes, it's no good to you now, then, Morris,' said the old man at last. 'What do you keep it for?'

The soldier shook his head. 'Fancy, I suppose,' he said slowly. 'I did have some idea of selling it, but I don't think I will. It has caused enough mischief already. Besides, people won't buy. They think it's a fairy tale, some of them; and those who do think anything of it want to try it first and pay me afterwards.'

'If you could have another three wishes,' said the old man, eyeing him keenly, 'would you have them?'

'I don't know,' said the other. 'I don't know.'

He took the paw, and dangling it between his forefinger and thumb, suddenly threw it upon the fire. White, with a slight cry, stooped down and snatched it off.

'Better let it burn,' said the soldier solemnly.

'If you don't want it, Morris,' said the other, 'give it to me.'

'I won't,' said his friend doggedly. 'I threw it on the fire. If you keep it, don't blame me for what happens. Pitch it on the fire again, like a sensible man.'

The other shook his head and examined his new possession closely. 'How do you do it?' he inquired.

'Hold it up in your right hand and wish aloud,' said the sergeant-major, 'but I warn you of the consequences.'

'Sounds like *Arabian Nights*,' said Mrs. White, as she rose and began to set the supper. 'Don't you think you might wish for four pairs of hands for me?'

Her husband drew the talisman from his pocket, and then all three burst into laughter as the sergeant-major, with a look of alarm on his face, caught him by the arm.

'If you must wish,' he said gruffly, 'wish for something sensible.'

Mr. White dropped it back in his pocket, and placing chairs, motioned his friend to the table. In the business of supper the talisman was partly forgotten, and afterwards the three sat listening in an enthralled fashion to a second instalment of the soldier's adventures in India.

'If the tale about the monkey's paw is not more truthful than those he has been telling us,' said Herbert, as the door closed behind their guest, just in time to catch the last train, 'we shan't get much out of it.'

'Did you give him anything for it, father?' inquired Mrs. White, regarding her husband closely.

'A trifle,' said he, colouring slightly. 'He didn't want it, but I made him take it. And he pressed me again to throw it away.'

'Likely,' said Herbert, with pretended horror. 'Why, we're going to be rich, and famous and happy. Wish to be an Emperor, father, to begin with; then you can't be henpecked.'

He darted round the table, pursued by the maligned Mrs. White with an antimacassar.

Mr. White took the paw from his pocket and eyed it dubiously. 'I don't know what to wish for, and that's a fact,' he said, slowly. 'It seems to me I've got all I want.'

'If you only cleared the house, you'd be quite happy, wouldn't you?' said Herbert, with his hand on his shoulder. 'Well, wish for two hundred pounds then; that'll just do it.'

His father, smiling shamefacedly at his own credulity, held up the talisman, as his son, with a solemn face, somewhat marred by a wink at his mother, sat down at the piano and struck a few impressive chords.

'I wish for two hundred pounds,' said the old man distinctly.

A fine crash from the piano greeted the words, interrupted by a shuddering cry from the old man. His wife and son ran towards him.

'It moved,' he cried, with a glance of disgust at the object as it lay on the floor.

'As I wished, it twisted in my hand like a snake.'

'Well, I don't see the money,' said his son, as he picked it up and placed it on the table, 'and I bet I never shall.'

'It must have been your fancy, father,' said his wife, regarding him anxiously.

He shook his head. 'Never mind, though; there's no harm done, but it gave me a shock all the same.'

They sat down by the fire again while the two men finished their pipes. Outside, the wind was higher than ever, and the old man started nervously at the sound of a door banging upstairs. A silence unusual and depressing settled upon all three, which lasted until the old couple arose to retire for the night.

'I expect you'll find the cash tied up in a big bag in the middle of your bed,' said Herbert, as he bade them good night, 'and something horrible squatting up on top of your wardrobe watching you as you pocket your ill-gotten gains.'

He sat alone in the darkness, gazing at the dying fire, and seeing faces in it. The last face was so horrible and so simian that he gazed at it in amazement. It got so vivid that, with a little uneasy laugh, he felt on the table for a glass containing a little water to throw over it. His hand grasped the monkey's paw, and with a little shiver he wiped his hand on his coat and went up to bed.

In the brightness of the wintry sun next morning as it streamed over the breakfast table, he laughed at his fears. There was an air of prosaic wholesomeness about the room which it had lacked on the previous night, and the dirty, shrivelled little paw was pitched on the sideboard with a carelessness which betokened no great belief in its virtues.

'I suppose all old soldiers are the same,' said Mrs. White. 'The idea of our listening to such nonsense! How could wishes be granted in these days? And if they could, how could two hundred pounds hurt you, father?'

'Might drop on his head from the sky,' said the frivolous Herbert.

'Morris said the things happened so naturally,' said his father, 'that you might if you so wished attribute it to coincidence.'

'Well, don't break into the money before I come back,' said Herbert as he rose from the table. 'I'm afraid it'll turn you into a mean, avaricious man, and we shall have to disown you.'

His mother laughed, and following him to the door, watched him down the road; and returning to the breakfast table, was very merry at the expense of her husband's credulity. All of which did not prevent her from scurrying to the door at the postman's knock, nor prevent her from referring somewhat shortly to retired sergeant-majors of bibulous habits when she found that the post brought a tailor's bill.

'Herbert will have some more of his funny remarks, I expect, when he comes home,' she said, as they sat at dinner.

'I dare say,' said Mr. White, pouring himself out some beer; 'but for all that, the thing moved in my hand; that I'll swear to.'

'You thought it did,' said the old lady soothingly.

'I say it did,' replied the other. 'There was no thought about it; I had just – What's the matter?'

His wife made no reply. She was watching the mysterious movements of a man outside, who, peering in an undecided fashion at the house, appeared to be trying to make up his mind to enter. In mental connexion with the two hundred pounds, she noticed that the stranger was well dressed, and wore a silk hat of glossy newness. Three times he paused at the gate, and then walked on again. The fourth time he stood with his hand upon it, and then with sudden resolution flung it open and walked up the path. Mrs. White at the same moment placed her hands behind her, and hurriedly unfastening the strings of her apron, put that useful article of apparel beneath the cushion of her chair.

She brought the stranger, who seemed ill at ease, into the room. He gazed at her furtively, and listened in a preoccupied fashion as the old lady apologized for the appearance of the room, and her husband's coat, a garment which he usually reserved for the garden. She then waited as patiently as her sex would permit, for him to broach his business, but he was at first strangely silent.

'I – was asked to call,' he said at last, and stooped and picked a piece of cotton from his trousers. 'I come from "Maw and Meggins".'

The old lady started. 'Is anything the matter?' she asked breathlessly. 'Has anything happened to Herbert? What is it?'

Her husband interposed. 'There, there, mother,' he said hastily. 'Sit down and don't jump to conclusions. You've not brought bad news, I'm sure, sir;' and he eyed the other wistfully.

'I'm sorry –' began the visitor.

'Is he hurt?' demanded the mother wildly.

The visitor bowed in assent. 'Badly hurt,' he said quietly, 'but he is not in any pain.'

'Oh, thank God!' said the old woman, clasping her hands. 'Thank God for that! Thank –'

She broke off suddenly as the sinister meaning of the assurance dawned upon her, and she saw the awful confirmation of her fears in the other's averted face. She caught her breath, and turning to her slower-witted husband, laid her trembling old hand upon his. There was a long silence.

'He was caught in the machinery,' said the visitor at length in a low voice.

'Caught in the machinery,' repeated Mr. White in a dazed fashion, 'yes.'

He sat staring blankly out at the window, and taking his wife's hand between his own, pressed it as he had been wont to do in their old courting days nearly forty years before.

'He was the only one left to us,' he said, turning gently to the visitor. 'It is hard.'

The other coughed, and rising, walked slowly to the window. 'The firm wished me to convey their sincere sympathy with you in your great loss,' he said without looking round. 'I beg that you will understand I am only their servant and merely obeying orders.'

There was no reply; the old woman's face was white, her eyes staring, and her breath inaudible; and on the husband's face was a look such as his friend the sergeant might have carried into his first action.

'I was to say that Maw and Meggins disclaim all responsibility,' continued the other. 'They admit no liability at all, but in consideration of your son's services, they wish to present you with a certain sum as compensation.'

Mr. White dropped his wife's hand, and rising to his feet, gazed with a look of horror at his visitor. His dry lips shaped the words, 'How much?'

'Two hundred pounds,' was the answer.

Unconscious of his wife's shriek, the old man smiled faintly, put out his hands like a sightless man, and dropped, a senseless heap, to the floor.

In the huge cemetery, some miles distant, the old people buried their dead, and came back to a house steeped in shadow and silence. It was all over so quickly that at first they could hardly realize it, and remained in a state of expectation as though of something else to happen – something else which was to lighten this load, too heavy for old hearts to bear.

But the days passed, and expectation gave place to resignation – the hopeless resignation of the old, sometimes miscalled apathy. Sometimes, they hardly exchanged a word, for now they had nothing to talk about, and their days were long to weariness.

It was about a week after, that the old man, waking suddenly in the night, stretched out his hand and found himself alone. The room was in darkness, and the sound of subdued weeping came from the window. He raised himself in bed and listened.

'Come back,' he said, tenderly. 'You will be cold.'

'It is colder for my son,' said the old woman, and wept afresh.

The sound of her sobs died away on his ears. The bed was warm, and his eyes heavy with sleep. He dozed fitfully and then slept until a sudden wild cry from his wife awoke him with a start.

'*The paw!*' she cried wildly. 'The monkey's paw!'

He started up in alarm. 'Where? Where is it? What's the matter?'

She came stumbling across the room towards him. 'I want it,' she said quietly. 'You've not destroyed it?'

'It's in the parlour, on the bracket,' he replied, marvelling. 'Why?'

She cried and laughed together, and bending over, kissed his cheek.

'I only just thought of it,' she said, hysterically. 'Why didn't I think of it before? Why didn't *you* think of it?'

'Think of what?' he questioned.

'The other two wishes,' she replied, rapidly. 'We've only had one.'

'Was not that enough?' he demanded fiercely.

'No,' she cried triumphantly; 'we'll have one more. Go down and get it quickly, and wish our boy alive again.'

The man sat up in bed and flung the bedclothes from his quaking limbs. 'Good God, you are mad!' he cried aghast.

'Get it,' she panted, 'get it quickly, and wish – Oh, my boy, my boy!'

Her husband struck a match and lit the candle. 'Get back to bed,' he said unsteadily. 'You don't know what you are saying.'

'We had the first wish granted,' said the old woman, feverishly; 'why not the second?'

'A coincidence,' stammered the old man.

'Go and get it and wish,' cried his wife, quivering with excitement.

The old man turned and regarded her, and his voice shook. 'He has been dead ten days, and besides he – I would not tell you else, but – I could only recognize him by his clothing. If he was too terrible for you to see then, how now?'

'Bring him back,' cried the old woman, and dragged him towards the door. 'Do you think I fear the child I have nursed?'

He went down in the darkness, and felt his way to the parlour, and then to the mantelpiece. The talisman was in its place, and a horrible fear that the unspoken wish might bring his mutilated son before him ere he could escape from the room seized upon him, and he caught his breath as he found that he had lost the direction of the door. His brow cold with sweat, he felt his way round the table, and groped along the wall until he found himself in the small passage with the unwholesome thing in his hand.

Even his wife's face seemed changed as he entered the room. It was white and expectant, and to his fears seemed to have an unnatural look upon it. He was afraid of her.

'*Wish,*' she cried in a strong voice.

'It is foolish and wicked,' he faltered.

'*Wish!*' repeated his wife.

He raised his hand. 'I wish my son alive again.'

The talisman fell to the floor, and he regarded it fearfully. Then he sank trembling into a chair as the old woman, with burning eyes, walked to the window and raised the blind.

He sat until he was chilled with the cold, glancing occasionally at the figure of the old woman peering through the window. The candle-end, which had burned below the rim of the china candlestick, was throwing pulsating shadows on the ceiling and walls, until, with a flicker larger than the rest, it expired. The old man, with an unspeakable sense of relief at the failure of the talisman, crept back to his bed, and a minute or two afterwards the old woman came silently and apathetically beside him.

Neither spoke, but lay silently listening to the ticking of the clock. A stair creaked, and a squeaky mouse scurried noisily through the wall. The darkness was oppressive, and after lying for some time, screwing up his courage, he took the box of matches, and striking one, went downstairs for a candle.

At the foot of the stairs the match went out, and he paused to strike another; and at the same moment a knock, so quiet and stealthy as to be scarcely audible, sounded on the front door.

The matches fell from his hand and spilled in the passage. He stood motionless, his breath suspended until the knock was repeated. Then he turned and fled swiftly back to his room, and closed the door behind him. A third knock sounded through the house.

'*What's that?*' cried the old woman, starting up.

'A rat,' said the old man in shaking tones, '– a rat. It passed me on the stairs.'

His wife sat up in bed listening. A loud knock resounded through the house.

'It's Herbert!' she screamed. 'It's Herbert!'

She ran to the door, but her husband was before her, and catching her by the arm, held her tightly.

'What are you going to do?' he whispered hoarsely.

'It's my boy; it's Herbert!' she cried, struggling mechanically. 'I forgot it was two miles away. What are you holding me for? Let go. I must open the door.'

'For God's sake don't let it in,' cried the old man, trembling.

'You're afraid of your own son,' she cried, struggling. 'Let me go. I'm coming, Herbert; I'm coming.'

There was another knock, and another. The old woman with a sudden wrench broke free and ran from the room. Her husband followed to the landing, and called after her appealingly as she hurried downstairs. He heard the chain rattle back and the bottom bolt drawn slowly and stiffly from the socket. Then the old woman's voice, strained and panting.

'The bolt,' she cried loudly. 'Come down. I can't reach it.'

But her husband was on his hands and knees groping wildly on the floor in search of the paw. If he could only find it before the thing outside got in. A perfect fusillade of knocks reverberated through the house, and he heard the scraping of a chair as his wife put it down in the passage against the door. He heard the creaking of the bolt as it came slowly back, and at the same moment he found the monkey's paw, and frantically breathed his third and last wish.

The knocking ceased suddenly, although the echoes of it were still in the house. He heard the chair drawn back, and the door opened. A cold wind rushed up the staircase, and a long loud wail of disappointment and misery from his wife gave him the courage to run down to her side, and then to the gate beyond. The street lamp flickering opposite shone on a quiet and deserted road.

The Seventh Pullet
Saki

Saki was the pseudonym of Hector Hugh Munroe. He was born in Burma, in 1870, the son of a police official, but was brought up by Aunts, in Devon. In much of his writings can be found a reaction to his strict upbringing. Invalided out of the Burma police, he took up journalism and writing in London. In the First World War he served as a private, having refused a commission, and was killed in action in 1916.

'It's not the daily grind that I complain of,' said Blenkinthrope resentfully; 'it's the dull grey sameness of my life outside of office hours. Nothing of interest comes my way, nothing remarkable or out of the common. Even the little things that I do try to find some interest in don't seem to interest other people. Things in my garden, for instance.'

'The potato that weighed just over two pounds,' said his friend Gorworth.

'Did I tell you about that?' said Blenkinthrope; 'I was telling the others in the train this morning. I forgot if I'd told you.'

'To be exact you told me that it weighed just under two pounds, but I took into account the fact that abnormal vegetables and freshwater fish have an after-life, in which growth is not arrested.'

'You're just like the others,' said Blenkinthrope sadly, 'you only make fun of it.'

'The fault is with the potato, not with us,' said Gorworth; 'we are not in the least interested in it because it is not in the least interesting. The men you go up in the train with every day are just in the same case as yourself; their lives are commonplace and not very interesting to themselves, and they certainly are not going to wax enthusiastic over the commonplace events in other men's lives. Tell them something startling, dramatic, piquant, that has happened to yourself or to some one in your family, and you will capture their interest at once. They will talk about you with a certain personal pride to all their acquaintances. "Man I know intimately, fellow called Blenkinthrope, lives down my way, had two of his fingers clawed clean off by a lobster he was carrying home to supper. Doctor says entire hand may have to come off." Now that is conversation of a very high order. But imagine walking into a tennis club with the remark: "I know a man who has grown a potato weighing two and a quarter pounds." '

'But hang it all, my dear fellow,' said Blenkinthrope impatiently, 'haven't I just told you that nothing of a remarkable nature ever happens to me?'

'Invent something,' said Gorworth. Since winning a prize for excellence in Scriptural knowledge at a preparatory school he had felt licensed to be a little more unscrupulous than the circle he moved in. Much might surely be excused to one who in early life could give a list of seventeen trees mentioned in the Old Testament.

'What sort of thing?' asked Blenkinthrope, somewhat snappishly.

'A snake got into your hen-run yesterday morning and killed six out of seven pullets, first mesmerizing them with its eyes and then biting them as they stood helpless. The seventh pullet was one of that French sort, with feathers all over its eyes, so it escaped the mesmeric snare, and just flew at what it could see of the snake and pecked it to pieces.'

'Thank you,' said Blenkinthrope stiffly; 'it's a very clever invention. If such a thing had really happened in my poultry-run I admit I should have been proud and interested to tell people about it. But I'd rather stick to fact, even if it is plain fact.' All the same his mind dwelt wistfully on the story of the Seventh Pullet. He could picture himself telling it in the train amid the absorbed interest of his fellow-passengers. Unconsciously all sorts of little details and improvements began to suggest themselves.

Wistfulness was still his dominant mood when he took his seat in the railway carriage the next morning. Opposite him sat Stevenham, who had attained to a recognized brevet of importance through the fact of an uncle having dropped dead in the act of voting at a Parliamentary election. That had happened three years ago, but Stevenham was still deferred to on all questions of home and foreign politics.

'Hullo, how's the giant mushroom, or whatever it was?' was all the notice Blenkinthrope got from his fellow-travellers.

Young Duckby, whom he mildly disliked, speedily monopolized the general attention by an account of a domestic bereavement.

'Had four pigeons carried off last night by a whacking big rat. Oh, a monster he must have been; you could tell by the size of the hole he made breaking into the loft.'

No moderate-sized rate ever seemed to carry out any predatory operations in these regions; they were all enormous in their enormity.

'Pretty hard lines that,' continued Duckby, seeing that he had secured the attention and respect of the company; 'four squeakers carried off at one swoop. You'd find it rather hard to match that in the way of unlooked-for bad luck.'

'I had six pullets out of a pen of seven killed by a snake yesterday afternoon,' said Blenkinthrope, in a voice which he hardly recognized as his own.

'By a snake?' came in excited chorus.

'It fascinated them with its deadly, glittering eyes, one after the other, and struck them down while they stood helpless. A bedridden neighbour, who wasn't able to call for assistance, witnessed it all from her bedroom window.'

'Well, I never!' broke in the chorus, with variations.

'The interesting part of it is about the seventh pullet, the one that didn't get killed,' resumed Blenkinthrope, slowly lighting a cigarette. His diffidence had left him, and he was beginning to realise how safe and easy depravity can seem once one has the courage to begin. 'The six dead birds were Minorcas; the seventh was a Houdan with a mop of feathers all over its eyes. It could hardly see the snake at all, so of course, it wasn't mesmerised like the others. It just could see something wriggling on the ground, and went for it and pecked it to death.'

'Well, I'm blessed!' exclaimed the chorus.

In the course of the next few days Blenkinthrope discovered how little the loss of one's self-respect affects one when one has gained the esteem of the world. His story found its way into one of the poultry papers, and was copied thence into a daily news-sheet as a matter of general interest. A lady wrote from the North of Scotland recounting a similar episode which she had witnessed as occurring between a stoat and a blind grouse. Somehow a lie seems so much less reprehensible when one can call it a lee.

For a while the adapter of the Seventh Pullet story enjoyed to the full his altered standing as a person of consequence, one who had had some share in the strange events of his times. Then he was thrust once again into the cold grey background by the sudden blossoming into importance of Smith-Paddon, a daily fellow-traveller, whose little girl had been knocked down and nearly hurt by a car belonging to a musical-comedy actress. The actress was not in the car at the time, but she was in numerous photographs which appeared in the illustrated papers of Zoto Dobreen inquiring after the well-being of Maisie, daughter of Edmund Smith-Paddon, Esq. With this new human interest to absorb them the travelling companions were almost rude when Blenkinthrope tried to explain his contrivance for keeping vipers and peregrine falcons out of his chicken-run.

Gorworth, to whom he unburdened himself in private, gave him the same counsel as theretofore.

'Invent something.'

'Yes, but what?'

The ready affirmative coupled with the question betrayed a significant shifting of the ethical standpoint.

It was a few days later that Blenkinthrope revealed a chapter of family history to the customary gathering in the railway carriage.

'Curious thing happened to my aunt, the one who lives in Paris,' he began. He had several aunts, but they were all geographically distributed over Greater London.

'She was sitting on a seat in the Bois the other afternoon, after lunching at the Roumanian Legation.'

Whatever the story gained in picturesqueness for the dragging-in of diplomatic 'atmosphere,' it ceased from that moment to command any acceptance as a record of current events. Gorworth had warned his neophyte that this would be the case, but the traditional enthusiasm of the neophyte had triumphed over discretion.

'She was feeling rather drowsy, the effect probably of the champagne, which she's not in the habit of taking in the middle of the day.'

A subdued murmur of admiration went round the company. Blenkinthrope's aunts were not used to taking champagne in the middle of the year, regarding it exclusively as a Christmas and New Year accessory.

'Presently a rather portly gentleman passed by her seat and paused an instant to light a cigar. At that moment a youngish man came up behind him, drew the blade from a swordstick, and stabbed him half a dozen times through and through. "Scoundrel," he cried to his victim, "you do not know me. My name is Henri Leturc.' The elder man wiped away some of the blood that was spattering his clothes, turned to his assailant, and said: "And since when has an attempted assassination been considered an introduction?" Then he finished lighting his cigar and walked away. My aunt had intended screaming for the police, but seeing the indifference with which the principal in the affair treated the matter she felt that it would be an impertinence on her part to interfere. Of course I need hardly say she put the whole thing down to the effects of a warm, drowsy afternoon and the Legation champagne. Now comes the astonishing part of my story. A fortnight later a bank manager was stabbed to death with a sword-stick in that very part of the Bois. His assassin was the son of a charwoman formerly working at the bank, who had been dismissed from her job by the manager on account of chronic intemperance. His name was Henri Leturc.'

From that moment Blenkinthrope was tacitly accepted as the Munchausen of the party. No effort was spared to draw him out from day to day in the exercise of testing their powers of credulity, and Blenkinthrope, in the false security of an assured and receptive audience, waxed industrious and ingenious in supplying the demand for marvels. Duckby's satirical story of a tame otter that had a tank in the garden to swim in, and whined restlessly whenever the water-rate was overdue, was scarcely an unfair parody of some of Blenkinthrope's wilder efforts. And then one day came Nemesis.

Returning to his villa one evening Blenkinthrope found his wife sitting in front of a pack of cards, which she was scrutinising with unusual concentration.

'The same old patience-game?' he asked carelessly.

'No, dear; this is the Death's Hand patience, the most difficult of them all. I've never got it to work out, and somehow I should be rather frightened if I did. Mother only got it out once in her life; she was afraid of it, too. Her great-aunt had done it once and fallen dead from excitement the next moment, and mother always had a feeling that she would die if she ever got it out. She died the same night that she did it. She was in bad health at the time, certainly, but it was a strange coincidence.'

'Don't do it if it frightens you,' was Blenkinthrope's practical comment as he left the room. A few minutes later his wife called to him.

'John, it gave me such a turn, I nearly got it out. Only the five of diamonds held me up at the end. I really thought I'd done it.'

'Why, you can do it,' said Blenkinthrope, who had come back to the room; 'if you shift the eight of clubs on to that open nine the five can be moved on to the six.'

His wife made the suggested move with hasty, trembling fingers, and piled the outstanding cards on to their respective packs. Then she followed the example of her mother and great-grand-aunt.

Blenkinthrope had been genuinely fond of his wife, but in the midst of his bereavement one dominant thought obtruded itself. Something sensational and real had at last come into his life; no longer was it a grey, colourless record. The headlines which might appropriately describe his domestic tragedy kept shaping themselves in his brain. 'Inherited presentiment comes true.' 'The Death's Head patience: Card-game that justified its sinister name in three generations.' He wrote out a full story of the fatal occurrence for the *Essex Vedette*, the editor of which was a friend of his, and to another friend he gave a condensed account, to be taken up to the office of one of the halfpenny dailies. But in both cases his reputation as a romancer stood fatally in the way of the fulfilment of his ambitions. 'Not the right thing to be Munchausening in a time of sorrow,' agreed his friends among themselves, and a brief note of regret at the 'sudden death of the wife of our respected neighbour, Mr John Blenkinthrope, from heart failure,' appearing in the news column of the local paper was the forlorn outcome of his visions of widespread publicity.

Blenkinthrope shrank from the society of his erstwhile travelling companions and took to travelling townwards by an earlier train. He sometimes tries to enlist the sympathy and attention of a chance acquaintance in details of the whistling prowess of his best canary or the dimensions of his largest beetroot; he scarcely recognises himself as the man who was once spoken about and pointed out as the owner of the Seventh Pullet.

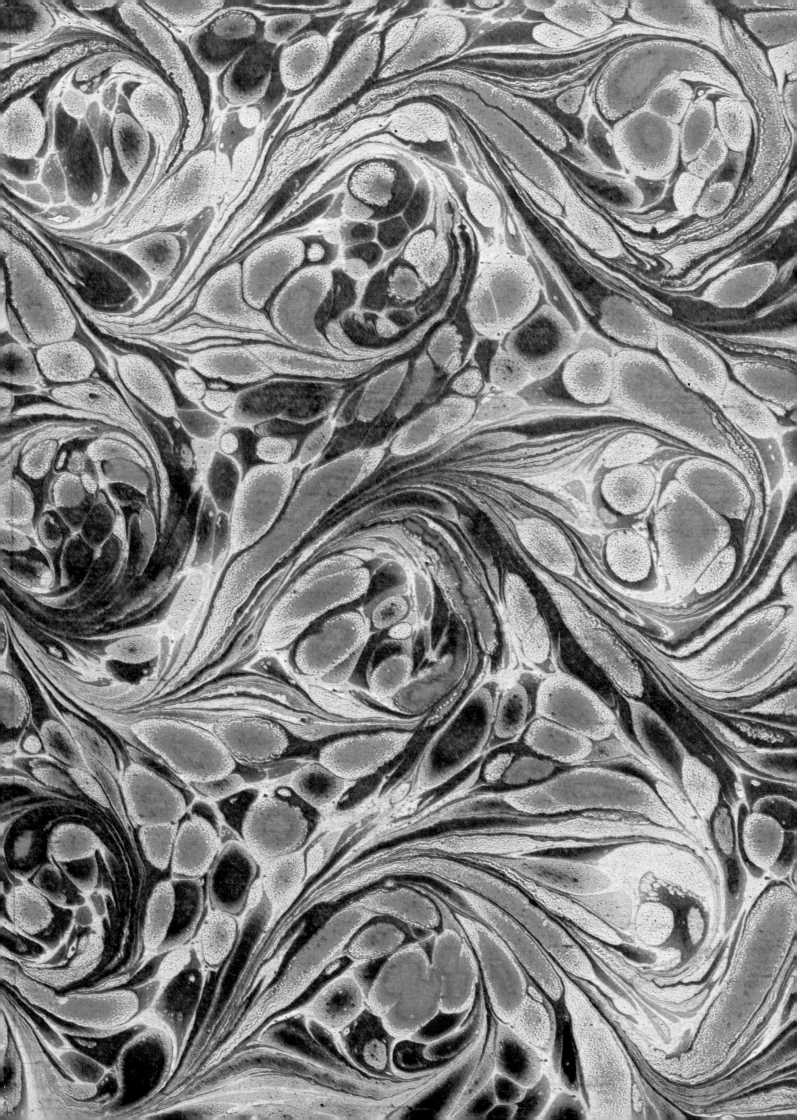